RABBOUNI

POCKETFUL OF

RAINBOWS

by

JOHN COGLIANO

Cover Illustration by Jake Rich

ISBN: 978-0-578-74518-3

To Liga, my wife and best friend

In Memory

of

my mother, Nell

Acknowledgements

Special thanks to the following: Lexie Stack, Vanessa Singleton, Austin Stack, Patrice Adams, and Marguerite Cogliano.

RABBOUNI

POCKETFUL OF

RAINBOWS

Chapter One

It was early Tuesday morning mid-September in New York City.

A young girl skipped down the sidewalk of a busy city street. She

was wearing a dark-blue plaid skirt that was one inch above her

knee, a powder-blue oxford dress shirt, and shiny black patent

leather shoes. She had earbuds on that were connected by a wire to

her backpack that hung from her shoulders. Her name was Ava

Marie Rose, and she was eight years old with blonde hair and

green eyes. A long shiny ball chain with two small rectangular

metal military identification tags swung from her neck as she sang

the Elvis Presley song "Pocketful of Rainbows". A purple

hummingbird zoomed in front of Ava letting out a sharp squeaky

chirping sound as it hovered in place causing her to abruptly stop.

At that moment, a large red object unexpectedly appeared in front of her as she teetered on the edge of the curb. She caught her balance as an old pickup truck, overloaded with construction equipment and too many dents to count, raced by within inches of hitting her as it made a left turn at the intersection. The hummingbird raced away. Ava grabbed the two metal identification tags with black rubber edges that hung from her neck and breathed a sigh of relief. "Whoa–thanks, Dad," she said then looked over toward the driver and said, "Sorry." The driver's face couldn't be seen as the pickup truck drove away with dirty exhaust spewing out of its tailpipe.

She looked both ways then darted across the street toward the massive gray stone cathedral that loomed over the intersection. The one-hundred-year-old Romanesque-Byzantine style structure occupied most of a city block. Its tall spires protruding from the twin bell towers seemed to pierce the sky. Ava ran up the stone stairs and removed her earbuds. She disappeared into one of the three enormous double-wooden doors, darkened from age, located at the front of the church.

The old hinges quietly cried out as the huge door slowly closed behind her. A self-standing wooden sign read: 7:00 AM Daily Service. She quickly walked through the narthex and into the cavernous nave that was six hundred feet long. Two rows of enormous white stone columns lined the length of the structure. Each column was the size of a full-grown redwood tree that stretched more than a hundred feet up to the ceiling. Even though she walked on the balls of her feet in an attempt to silence her footsteps, the muted echo still could be heard in the dimly lit hallowed chamber. There were a dozen other people scattered throughout the sanctuary. Only their bowed heads could be seen across the many empty wooden benches like a chain of distant islands from high above the open sea. Ava sat down on a wooden bench a few rows from the front of the middle section. She slipped her backpack off her shoulders and knelt down on the padded kneeler. She clasped her two hands together and prayed silently until the service began.

Forty-five minutes later, one of the large wooden double doors swung open and Ava emerged from inside the church. She ran down the steps and onto the sidewalk. A few blocks away, she stopped near a homeless man who was wrapped in a blanket and propped against a wall near the service entrance of a building.

"Excuse me, here's something for you," Ava said as she held out a folded dollar bill.

The homeless man had an unkempt beard with wisps of gray hair. He slowly opened his blurry blue eyes and tried to focus on Ava. "Huh…what'dya want?" the homeless man struggled to say.

"Here–this is for you," Ava said as she held the dollar out and stepped closer to him.

"Are you an angel?"

"No," Ava giggled as she held the dollar in front of his eyes.

"What's this?" the homeless man said as his trembling hand reached for the dollar bill.

"Just a little something."

The homeless man sat up and attempted to straighten himself up for her. Within a few moments he realized that there was nothing he could do to change his appearance. He slumped back against the wall then abashedly looked up toward Ava.

"Thanks—that's very kind of you," the homeless man said as he slowly took the dollar bill from her small hand. For a brief moment his response revealed what type of person he possibly once was before his present situation.

"I'll try to do more next time," Ava said as she smiled and waved goodbye.

The homeless man raised his gnarly hand and moved it side to side as she walked away. Ava took several steps, turned around and went back to him. She slipped off her backpack and unzipped it. She handed him a peanut butter and jelly sandwich sealed in a plastic bag and a juice box. Moments later, she was skipping down the sidewalk while singing that same Elvis song again.

Ava dodged the various people that crowded the sidewalk for their morning commute. A young man panhandling was standing in the middle of the sidewalk holding a paper coffee cup asking for money. A crudely scrawled cardboard sign hung from his neck that read: Homeless Veteran PLEASE HELP. She stopped a few feet from him and dug out the remaining money in her backpack. Ava walked over to him and dropped two quarters into his coffee cup. Each coin could be heard as it fell onto a thin layer of coins. "I hope you have a great day," Ava said as she handed him an apple. He was surprised by her generosity and stared at the apple for a few moments before looking up to say something to her. However, she had already skipped away before he could speak to her.

Ava made her way down the sidewalk through the fast-moving throng of people. She came upon an opening in the crowd at a cross street. A young man walking fast began to trot across the street toward Ava as she skipped off the curb and into the street toward him. He looked at Ava then his eyes darted to the left then back to her as he rushed at her. He pushed her back to the curb and into the group of people standing there. A red pickup truck, overloaded with construction equipment, hit the young man sending him upward. The crowd gasped. The pickup truck continued through the intersection as the young man hit the pavement fifteen feet away from the impact. His eyes were closed as he laid motionless on the ground. The crowd quickly gathered around him. One person yelled out for someone to call for help. Another asked if anyone saw the license plate number on the pickup truck. Ava walked over close enough to see the young man lying in the street. She folded her hands and bowed her head in prayer. She softly whispered three phrases three times, and on the very last word, the crowd gasped again. Then the crowd cheered followed by clapping and few loud whistles. The young man had regained consciousness; he sat up, then stood up and walked unaided to the sidewalk.

Ava was breathing hard, her legs were tired, as she ran around the corner and down the side street. The entrance to Fontbonne

Academy was still a hundred feet away. The school consisted of several red brick buildings that were connected in a way that resembled a fortress. A ten-foot-high brick wall surrounded the facility. She ran as fast as she could to the heavy metal door that was now closing. "Wait, Mr. Brown! Hold the door!" Ava yelled with every precious particle of air left in her lungs. The windowless metal door slammed shut with a dull thud. Then it immediately swung back open revealing a large framed man that stood six foot-five inches tall. It was Mr. Brown who handled the building maintenance at the school. He was dressed in dark-blue khaki pants and matching shirt. A large brass ring of keys hung from his aged-worn black leather belt. Mr. Brown held the door open with his outstretched arm. "Hurry up, Ava. Homeroom bell is gonna ring soon," Mr. Brown said as Ava ran past him.

"Thank you, Mr. Brown," Ava said as she tried to catch her breath. Mr. Brown pulled the heavy metal door closed as he went up a few steps then lifted Ava up by her extended arms to the next landing where she continued running down the empty hallway. She slid to a stop at the classroom door that was halfway down the hallway. Ava opened the door and entered the classroom filled with boys and girls sitting at their desks. The girls were all dressed the same as Ava with dark-blue plaid skirts and powder-blue oxford dress shirts. The boys were all dressed the same in dark-blue pants and powder-blue dress shirts. One girl said, "Ava made it." A boy sitting in the first seat of the row closest to the door motioned for Ava to move faster. The homeroom bell rang throughout the school.

"Ava Marie Rose–you're tardy! Go to the principal's office," Mr. Fred McCardin snapped as Ava stopped at her desk with her backpack on.

"Yes–Mr. McCardin," Ava said as she turned and walked to the door.

Ava, with her hands folded on her lap, was sitting on a wooden bench outside the principal's office. The first period bell rang through the empty hallway. The sound of spongy footsteps on the heavily polished wooden floor could be heard coming down the hallway. A lean, serious looking woman in her sixties walked towards Ava. She was wearing a black robe and had a black habit on her head. A wooden chain with small links hung from her neck to her sternum. It had a wooden cross at the bottom of the chain that swung side to side as she walked. Ava smiled at her as she approached the entrance to the principal's office.

"Good morning, Sister Eunice," Ava said.

"Good morning, Ava," Sister Eunice said. "What are you doing here?"

"Mr. McCardin sent me to the principal's office for being tardy," Ava said.

"I was told that you were standing by your desk when the homeroom bell rang?" Sister Eunice asked.

"Yes, sister; I was," Ava answered.

"Okay my dear, you've been here long enough. Come with me now," Sister Eunice said as she held her hand out to Ava.

"But sister, don't I have to see Sister Carmella?" Ava asked as she stood up from the bench and reached for Sister Eunice's hand.

"I'll speak with Sister Carmella after class. She would agree that you will learn more in the classroom than on this bench," Sister Eunice said as she and Ava, holding hands, walked down the hallway. "Were you attending mass this morning?"

Ava nodded her head. "Yes, sister."

"Where did you go today?" Sister Eunice asked.

"Saint John the Divine," Ava said.

"Ava, that's so far away. It must be twenty blocks from your home," Sister Eunice said.

"It's so beautiful," Ava said looking up to Sister Eunice.

"We have beautiful churches and cathedrals for you to visit and they're closer. Our Lord will hear all of your concerns, praise, and prayers at our local church just as well. You don't have to go to a different church every day to talk to him. He will hear you anywhere you stop and pray," Sister Eunice said as a sixth-grade student walked toward them. "Mr. Donner, what are you doing out of class?"

"I have the attendance sheets," Bobby Donner, holding a folder of papers, said as he stopped walking.

"Very good, continue on with your assignment. Then back to class," Sister Eunice said as she turned back to Ava. Bobby Donner resumed walking down the hallway.

"I know sister, but I feel closer to God when I'm in a church," Ava said.

"You must always remember; he is with you always—no matter where you are," Sister Eunice said as she smiled and lovingly squeezed Ava's hand.

A man, late thirties, carrying a black nylon bag, was walking down the street. He was good looking with strong facial features. He had a short haircut style with early stages of it receding. He was near the entrance to Fontbonne Academy when an unexpected tap on the shoulder caused him to stumble his next step. He stopped and quickly turned around to see who it was. Standing there was a tall man in his forties who was casually dressed in blue jeans. He was holding a small tape recorder in the palm of his left hand while his right hand was extended out.

"James Fulton?" he asked.

"Yes," Fulton said as he switched his bag to his left hand.

"Monsignor Fulton, my name is Duval Lewis. I'm a reporter at the National Network. I would like to speak with you for a few minutes," Lewis said.

"I don't have anything to say," a visibly stunned Fulton said as he pulled his hand from Lewis' grasp.

"Why did you leave the Archdiocese?" Lewis asked.

"I'm on sabbatical–good-bye," Fulton said as he walked away. Lewis leaped forward and walked alongside him.

"Is it a loss of faith?!" Lewis asked, sternly.

"Just a sabbatical. Nothing more," Fulton said as he increased his pace to the school entrance. Fulton pressed the doorbell button that was to the right of the metal door.

"Will you be taking a position here? This is an Archdiocese school, isn't it?" Lewis asked.

"Who is it?" asked a person from the intercom speaker that was located above the doorbell button.

"James Fulton," Fulton said into the intercom then turned to Lewis. A buzzing sound could be heard as the door lock was released. "No, I will not be working here. Good-bye." Fulton opened the heavy metal door and stepped up to enter the school building when Lewis grabbed his arm.

"Did you leave because of any sexual misconduct?" Lewis asked.

Fulton's annoyed facial expression changed to an angry look as he pulled away from Lewis and closed the door shut behind him. Lewis removed a notepad from his jacket pocket and scribbled down the name of the school and the address.

Mr. McCardin was in the principal's office area pacing outside Sister Carmella's office door. Black lettering on the door read: Sister Carmella – Principal. The door opened, and before Mr. McCardin could rush in, James Fulton appeared in the doorway. After exchanging a greeting, Fulton passed by Mr. McCardin who then hurried into Sister Carmella's office.

"This is outrageous!" McCardin exclaimed as he stormed into her office.

"Good morning, Mr. McCardin," Sister Carmella said as she turned away from the window. She was in her late sixties, dark-brown eyes, and had a young-looking smooth skinned face. She was wearing a black robe and had a black habit on her head. She had a long wooden chain hanging from her neck with a wooden cross at the end of it.

"I can't run my class if I'm going to be undermined!" Mr. McCardin yelled.

"Mr. McCardin, my hearing is fine. Please lower your voice and calmly explain the situation that has brought you to a state of borderline rage," Sister Carmella said.

"I was progressively reprimanding a student with a perpetual problem of tardiness! I sent her to your office! When I came down to bring her into your office, it appears that Sister Eunice disregarded the infraction and undermined my position at the school," Mr. McCardin growled as he jabbed his finger into the air.

"Please identify which of our three hundred students you're speaking about," Sister Carmella said.

"Ava Marie Rose," Mr. McCardin snarled.

Sister Carmella nodded her head without making a comment.

"Yes, your precious, angelic–Ava Marie. She has been tardy close to every day since the school year began. She can't go through life late for everything! Need I remind you about the famous maxim: spare the rod, spoil the child!" Mr. McCardin exclaimed.

"We're about love, mercy, and understanding," Sister Eunice said as she entered the room. "Our mission is to provide a solid foundation of faith and education with gospel values to our students–not abandon them in an empty hallway!"

"We need to educate them—not coddle them! We need to prepare them for life," Mr. McCardin said.

"Mr. McCardin, you need to get out more and enjoy life," Sister Eunice said.

"That is rather humorous coming from someone who has been living a somewhat cloistered life," Mr. McCardin snapped.

"If I may, Mr. McCardin, repetitive tardiness is a serious matter, and if unchecked, could develop into a long-term issue as an adult. However, we must also consider all the effectuating factors. Ava's father is dead, and her mother has a terminal illness. So, in this particular case, for the child's well-being, we should be understanding," Sister Carmella said.

Although Sister Carmella's door was open, Ms. Logan, the Administrative Assistant, knocked on the door to interrupt the conversation. "Excuse me, Sister Carmella, someone from child services is here to speak with you."

"Child services? About what?" Sister Carmella asked.

"Ava Marie Rose," Ms. Logan said.

Sister Eunice looked at Sister Carmella who then looked directly at Mr. McCardin.

"She's been living unsupervised in her home since last week when her mother went into the hospital," Mr. McCardin said.

"YOU called child services?!" Sister Carmella asked, shocked and with an edge of disbelief.

"I did. It was the responsible thing to do and legally required because she is a minor," Mr. McCardin said, smugly.

"How dare you?!" Sister Eunice exclaimed. "Why didn't you tell us that she was alone at home?!"

"Mr. McCardin, that will be all for now. Please get back to your daily schedule," Sister Carmella said with an angry tone. Mr. McCardin left the room. Sister Eunice turned to Sister Carmella.

"They will try to take her," Sister Eunice whispered.

"I know they will try, but we will not allow that," Sister Carmella said.

"Ava can stay in my room upstairs. I'll sleep in the hallway," Sister Eunice said.

"We will not let them take her away," Sister Carmella said as she grabbed Sister Eunice's arm. They both smiled.

Ms. Logan escorted Ms. Prudence Pratt of the Division of Child Services into Sister Carmella's office. Ms. Pratt sat down next to Sister Eunice at one of the two chairs in front of Sister Carmella's desk. She was short, almost as wide as she was tall, and had a young boy's haircut. Her smile was different; it was quite strange. She had a large mouth with a propensity to smile. Her teeth were clearly shown but not for any pleasant or happy reason. Ms. Pratt opened her black leather folder and pulled out a pen. She looked up and smiled across the desk at Sister Carmella who sat confidently in her chair.

"It has come to our attention that your student–Ava Marie Rose has been living at home without any adult family supervision. As I am sure you recognize, that type of environment for a minor is most dangerous and is unlawful–it VIOLATES both city and state regulations," Ms. Pratt said as she referred to her notes throughout her comments and ended them with a toothy smile.

"It has just come to our attention, not more than five minutes ago, that we learned Ava's mother may have been readmitted to the hospital for treatment," Sister Carmella said.

"You see, it's a great thing that the Division of Child Services exists. It provides a wonderful safety net for the young ones that may otherwise slip through and become lost," Ms. Pratt said as she nodded and smiled.

"While her mother is recuperating at the hospital, Ava can stay here in our living quarters. We can provide her with her own room with a bed and a desk. She can eat her meals with us. We will, of course, speak with her mother at the hospital to get her approval for these temporary arrangements," Sister Carmella said.

"That's not possible. Her mother is incapacitated. She has been in a coma since last week," Ms. Pratt said as she began to smile awkwardly then stopped.

"Mother of God," Sister Eunice said as she covered her mouth. Ms. Pratt's awkward smile changed to an annoyed look.

Sister Carmella quickly picked up her telephone and pressed a button. "Ms. Logan, please bring in Ava Marie's file. Thank you," Sister Carmella said then hung up the telephone. There was a knock at the door. Ms. Logan entered the room carrying a folder and handed it to Sister Carmella. She opened the file and scanned it.

"The next of kin is Desirea Jordan, 4147 Lincoln Boulevard, Apartment 1, Venice, California. A telephone number was not provided," Sister Carmella said as she looked up from the folder.

"We tried contacting Ms. Jordan. She does not have a listed telephone number," Ms. Pratt said.

"How did you know that she was listed as the next of kin?" Sister Eunice asked.

Ms. Pratt attempted to hide her obvious annoyance with Sister Eunice by half-turning toward her. The source of this strong emotion was less from the actual question, but more from Sister Eunice's mere presence. "We went to the hospital and met with the appropriate authorities," Ms. Pratt said with a forced smile before turning back toward Sister Carmella.

"You continually reference 'We'–who's 'We'?" Sister Eunice asked.

"Various personnel from the Division of Child Services," Ms. Pratt said as her eyes grew wide, and she flashed a big idiotic smile. "During our meeting with the hospital authorities, no contact telephone number was found for Ms. Desirea Jordan."

"We will conduct a thorough review of our files for a telephone number," Sister Carmella said.

"That won't be necessary. We have already begun the secure and safety process for this case," Ms. Pratt said.

"What is the 'secure and safety process'?" Sister Carmella asked.

"WE," Ms. Pratt said then momentarily stopped, looked down before regaining her stilted composure. "The Division of Child Services will assume custody of the child until we can identify and properly assess any next of kin then determine what is in the best interest of the child," Ms. Pratt said.

"What's best for this child is to stay here until we can communicate with her mother or speak to the appropriate next of kin. She has experienced too many traumatic events in her young life. The last thing she needs is upheaval in her daily routine!" Sister Eunice said.

"We would prefer that this go smoothly and without incident," Ms. Pratt said.

"What are you proposing to do with Ava?" Sister Carmella asked.

"We will assume custody of her as soon as the necessary paperwork is completed–which I expect to happen by the end of school–today. You know, we need to follow our regulations and guidelines," Ms. Pratt said as a toothy wide-grin reappeared.

"Don't you need a court order?" Sister Eunice asked.

"Sister, I'm sure Ms. Pratt knows what is required," Sister Carmella said.

"If we have to, we will go to court to get an order from a judge. However, I wanted to handle this in a civil manner," Ms. Pratt said.

"Ms. Pratt, you have paperwork to attend to back at your office. We will look through our files for any additional information that could be helpful," Sister Carmella said.

"All right, if you'd like to, but that won't be necessary," Ms. Pratt said as she stood up.

Sister Eunice maintained a stern look as Sister Carmella nodded her head and said, "God bless you, Ms. Pratt."

"Good day," Ms. Pratt said as she left the room and could be heard exchanging insincere pleasantries with Ms. Logan in the outer office area.

"We're not letting them take Ava away?!" Sister Eunice asked in an exasperated whisper.

"Of course not," Sister Carmella said. "But we needed some time in order to save her."

Chapter Two

Fulton was staying in the guest room in the modest housing quarters for the nuns located on the top two floors of the Administration Building at Fontbonne Academy. His black nylon bag was on a portable luggage rack beside a small wooden dresser with three drawers. A small television with a digital-to-analog TV converter box and rabbit ears antenna sat on the dresser. A news video clip on the television reported a high number of deaths and widespread destruction in a war zone area in another part of the world. The television screen changed to a flickering snowy picture and a high volume hissing static sound. Fulton came out of the bathroom holding a face towel. He walked over to the television and changed the channel. The snowy picture and static remained on that channel as well as the next few channels that he tried. He shut off the television which made the screen turn black. Fulton took a step toward the bathroom then leaped back toward the television screen. He briefly saw an image that he clearly recognized. "Dear God," Fulton exclaimed in complete wonder as he sat down on the edge of the bed. The image turned blurry, but Fulton was sure of what he saw. Then the blurry screen transformed into another image for a moment. Fulton stared at it not recognizing what it meant. The image disappeared from the screen. Fulton stared at the blank television screen waiting for another image. There was a knock at his door. Fulton kept his eyes on the blank television screen as he walked backwards to the door. Upon reaching the door while still staring at the television screen Fulton said, "Yes?"

"Monsignor Fulton, Sister Carmella would like to see you in her office as soon as you're available. She said that it was most urgent," the unknown messenger said from the other side of the door.

"Okay. Please tell her I'll be right there. Thank you," Fulton said as he continued to stare at the television screen waiting for something to happen.

Fulton stood by the window in Sister Carmella's office looking out into the school courtyard. Sister Carmella was sitting at her desk.

"I have seen things at the Archdiocese that contradicts what is sacred in the gospel, and this doesn't sit well with me," Fulton said as he interlocked his fingers between his hands and rested them on the dark wooden windowsill. "There's no more passion in me. I'm just tired–even my faith is tired."

"I do not doubt your faith in God at all. I know you as well as a mother knows her very own child. You were six years old when you started school here. What I was saying is you're giving up the greatest opportunity to make things right in the Archdiocese. It's not your faith in God that upsets you–it's your faith in humans making decisions and those decisions contradict what we know from the Word of God," Sister Carmella said. "Give it some time. Think about it. Pray on it."

"So, you want me to take one of the students to California?" Fulton asked in order to change the topic of their conversation.

"To see her great-aunt who is the only living relative," Sister Carmella said. "But we have to get her out of here now; otherwise child services will take her away."

"Does the great-aunt know we're bringing her out there?" Fulton asked.

"No," Sister Carmella said.

Fulton turned away from the window and asked. "You haven't called her yet?"

"There's no number to call. No email address," Sister Carmella said.

"Do we know this person?" Fulton asked.

Sister Carmella shook her head and said, "No."

"So, we don't know if this person is capable of caring for her? What is the name of the student?" Fulton said as he took several steps toward the desk. "You know this great-aunt may have moved or not even be alive."

"Ms. Logan searched for her obituary; most likely, she's alive. The student's name is Ava Marie Rose," Sister Carmella said.

"Hmmm," Fulton said. He had enough on his mind and did not want to add anything more to it. "Are you sure about doing this?"

"What I'm sure of–is that YOU must take her there," Sister Carmella said.

"All the way to California–and WHY are you so sure about this?" Fulton asked.

"Because, last night, the Holy Mother appeared to me in my room and told me that you would be coming here this morning and that you would take the child by plane to California. None of it made sense to me last night. But you arrived here this morning unexpectedly and then child services showed up here to take her away. We have been given clear instructions," Sister Carmella said. Two quick rings from the telephone broke the silence. Sister Carmella picked up the telephone, listened for a moment and said, "Please send her in."

The door opened to the office and Ava entered.

"Good morning, Ava," Sister Carmella said as she came from behind her desk to meet her.

Fulton was visibly shaken when he saw Ava standing there. He quickly regained his usual calm composure.

"Good morning, Sister Carmella," Ava said with a smile.

"I would like you to meet someone very dear to me and a former student here. This is Monsignor Fulton. Monsignor–this is Ava Marie Rose," Sister Carmella said.

Ava shook his hand and they exchanged greetings. Fulton thought that she was a sweet well-mannered girl even when she asked him why he was not wearing the traditional white collar and black suit. Fulton told her that he was on vacation. Sister Carmella explained to Ava that Fulton would be escorting her to visit her great-aunt.

"I'll have to ask my mom, but she's at the hospital," Ava said.

"Your mother already provided direction regarding you. We have to take you to see your Aunt Desirea. You'll come back soon to see your mom. But now you must go with Monsignor Fulton to the airport. Okay, dear?" Sister Carmella said.

Ava nodded her head. Sister Carmella told her to go back to her classroom to gather her personal items. She left the room.

Sister Carmella held out an envelope toward Fulton. "If you're willing to go–here's a signed letter from me stating that you are escorting her to visit a family member," Sister Carmella said.

Fulton looked down at the envelope for a few seconds. He ran various scenarios through his mind on possible outcomes for this particular decision as he would in his position at the Archdiocese. He then took the letter from her and said, "I'll take her."

"Thank you, James. Ms. Logan has made the travel arrangements for both of you," Sister Carmella said as she hugged him, "God bless you."

"Just before I came down here, when I was up in the guest room, I shut off the TV–the screen went dark. Then two images appeared–I recognized the first one. The second image–I didn't know who it was until that little girl walked in here. I'm positive that was her face on the television screen upstairs," Fulton said as he pointed at the door that Ava had just used to leave the room.

Fulton went back upstairs to the guest room to retrieve his bag for the trip. Meanwhile, Ava returned to her classroom to get her backpack as the third period class ended. The students filed out of the classroom for a fifteen-minute recess break in the school yard. Ava walked down the hallway with Sister Eunice and the other students. The children's conversations echoed off the walls as they moved toward the foyer near the principal's office.

"We pray that you have a safe trip. We'll miss you, Ava, and we'll see you soon," Sister Eunice said as many of the children followed with a goodbye.

As Sister Eunice and the group of students reached the foyer, Ms. Pratt appeared with a heavy-set man with beady eyes and a bushy mustache. "She's got to be one of them. Get ready to grab her," Ms. Pratt said to the heavy-set man as she pointed to the group of students walking toward them. "We're here for Ava Marie Rose!" Ms. Pratt said to Sister Eunice as she held up a handful of papers.

Sister Eunice reached out and grabbed Ava's arm. Ava was frightened by Ms. Pratt. She stopped moving with the other children.

"There she is–get her!" Ms. Pratt said to the heavy-set man as she pointed to Ava. "Under chapter sixty-six, section six, the Division of Child Services orders you to turn Ava Marie Rose over to ME!" Ms. Pratt exclaimed to Sister Eunice as the heavy-set man advanced toward the students.

The children immediately formed a circle around Ava. Some of the children screamed for help while others yelled at the heavy-set man to stay away. Sister Eunice moved into the path of the advancing heavy-set man attempting to block him from reaching the children surrounding Ava.

"You have no authority to be here! Leave the school premises immediately!" Sister Eunice demanded as she held her hand up to the heavy-set man who stopped moving as he looked back to a waddling Ms. Pratt for instructions.

Sister Carmella rushed out of her office toward the foyer as Ms. Logan called the police.

"We do have the authority! Grab HER!" yelled Ms. Pratt. The heavy-set man pushed past Sister Eunice knocking her to the ground. The children and Ava stepped backwards. A few of the boy students confronted the heavy-set man.

"You're a bad man—you hit Sister Eunice!" Andrew Singleton shouted as he kicked the man in the shin. The heavy-set man winced then backhanded Andrew away. Keys could be heard jingling down the hallway. A man dressed in dark-blue clothing raced by Ms. Pratt and knocked the heavy-set man to the floor. It was Mr. Brown, and he followed the heavy-set man to the floor driving his knee into his back.

"What—you don't like kids?!" Mr. Brown growled.

"Ms. Pratt—how dare you barge in here and behave in this manner!" Sister Carmella exclaimed.

Two policemen, mid-thirties, stood in the hallway and listened to Sister Carmella explain what had happened. The policemen split up to question the various people involved in the incident. Fulton, holding his bag, stepped into the hallway perplexed with the chaotic scene. Sister Carmella motioned for him to walk toward the front entrance as she grabbed Ava by the hand and guided her through the crowded area. They walked down the stairs to the front door. Sister Carmella knelt down and hugged Ava.

"Will you come with us?" Ava softly asked her.

"No, dear. I'm sorry; I have to stay here. You'll be fine. Go with Monsignor Fulton to see your aunt. You'll be back here before you know it," Sister Carmella said then she kissed Ava on the forehead.

Fulton and Ava went out the front door and walked down the sidewalk. Duval Lewis was sitting on the stoop of a brownstone house across the street. He swung a leather satchel over his shoulder, ran down the stone steps, and followed them from a distance as they walked to the next intersection. Fulton raised his hand. A small yellow taxi pulled over to the curb. They slipped into the back seat then the taxi drove away. Lewis jogged to the curb and hailed a taxi. He reached for the handle of the rear door before it came to a complete stop. Lewis opened the door and leaped into the back seat. The taxi lurched forward then raced down the street.

The airport was crowded with travelers intently focused on moving through the various lines while others were milling about with their luggage. Lewis was positioned at a self-service check-in kiosk closest to the ticket counter. He pretended to search for a credit card in his wallet as he eavesdropped on the nearby conversation at the ticket counter. Fulton and Ava walked away from the ticket counter. Lewis rushed over to the counter cutting off several people who were already in que to be serviced. A businessman with several pieces of luggage stepped forward to confront Lewis on his rude behavior, but stopped when another ticket agent at the counter raised her hand as she announced for the next person in line. The businessman shook his head at Lewis and turned to the available ticket agent at the counter.

"I'm trying to get on the next flight to LA–same as those folks you just helped," Lewis said as he slid his credit card and license on the counter toward the ticket agent. "Thanks."

The ticket agent tapped away on her keyboard and said, "The next flight to LA landing at LAX airport–the only seat available is in first class at three thousand dollars–round trip." The ticket agent pursed her lips and wrinkled her nose as a sympathetic gesture to Lewis for the cost of the late purchase.

"I'll take it," Lewis said as he looked over to the security line and saw Fulton and Ava making their way through it.

"Okay, Mr. Lewis, that'll take just a few minutes," the ticket agent said as she processed the ticket.

"That little girl that was just here–she was so cute," Lewis said to the ticket agent. "He's lucky to have her for a daughter."

"Oh, yes–she was a cutie," the ticket agent said as she continued tapping on her keyboard. "But, he's not the father. He's just escorting her to a family member–I think it's an aunt. All right, here's your boarding pass."

Lewis walked away from the ticket counter with his smartphone to his ear and said into it, "Oh, yeah–I'm still following him. I'm at the airport now. Get this–he's taking a little girl from that school that he went into this morning–to frick'in LA! Why is the Vicar General of the Archdiocese of New York escorting some kid across the country?! Why did he unexpectedly go on a 'sabbatical' as he said to me? My sources inside told me that Fulton has been acting funny over the past several months. It doesn't make sense. Something's going on."

James Robert Fulton grew up in Hempstead, Long Island, New York in a modest house in a multi-ethnic middle-class neighborhood. Fulton was raised by his mother after his father left them as a result of his weakness for alcohol and women. His mother, Eugenia Foley, had grown up in South Boston, Massachusetts. It was the predominantly Irish section of the city that was known locally as Southie. She had met James' father, Robert Fulton, when she went with her mother on a mid-week two-day trip to New York City. It was her senior year in high school during the Christmas break in 1972. Eugenia, her mother, and grandmother went to see a few musical shows and do some shopping. It was at the Radio City Music Hall that she met Robert Fulton. He was twenty-four years old, tall, good looking, dark hair, blue eyes and was working as an usher during the matinee shows. Robert always said that he fell in love with Eugenia the moment that he set eyes on her which was when she handed him the three tickets to the Rockettes for the afternoon show. Eugenia was an attractive young lady with blond hair and green-hazel eyes. She appeared older because she was wearing her mother's clothes and jewelry.

During a trip to the ladies' bathroom by herself, Robert approached Eugenia and told her that he was madly in love with her. He confessed to her that if she wouldn't marry him; he'd rather not be alive. She was flattered and a little uneasy with his forwardness. However, after meeting him in the hotel lobby that night and his surprise visit the next morning at the bus station to see her off, she nervously gave him her address so they could write to each other. The scheduled five-hour bus ride to Boston took two hours longer as a result of a heavy snowfall that morning. The next afternoon Robert appeared at the front door of her home at 3080 West Third Street in South Boston.

Eugenia's father, Mr. Foley, made Robert stand outside the front door while she quickly fixed her hair. The day before Robert had abruptly quit his job at Radio City Music Hall and hitch-hiked rides north to Boston. He told Eugenia his life plans–he was now in Boston determined to marry her. Robert didn't care how long it took Eugenia to fall in love with him. He said they were meant for each other. He was here to stay. Eugenia was pleasantly moved by this romantic overture by this young man from New York that she had just met two days ago, and he left everything behind for her. She thought that it was just like something out of a movie. No one at South Boston High School had ever been pursued to this extreme. Nonetheless, Eugenia and her mother were cautious, very religious, and strongly advised Robert to slow down. Robert took a room at the L Street Bath House that was more like a closet and began doing odd jobs in the neighborhood. He eventually got a job as an insurance sales broker. Robert even attended weekly Sunday mass with the Foley's at the Gate of Heaven Church. Although Eugenia's mother and grandmother eventually warmed up to Robert, Mr. Foley never did and rarely spoke to him using as few words as humanly possible. After two years of courtship, Eugenia and Robert were married and soon after he took a sales position at a large insurance company in New York City requiring them to move to Hempstead, Long Island.

After James Robert Fulton was born in 1975, Robert began to stay out after work drinking and having dinner with clients and brokers that always led to entertaining women. Eugenia was suspicious of Robert's behavior; however, whether it was pride or her deep religious belief in the sanctity of marriage, they stayed together. Eugenia rarely complained or confronted Robert about the late evenings out or the overnight business trips without any telephone calls home. It wasn't until Robert came home and told Eugenia that he was divorcing her that fourteen-year-old James learned that there was any trouble between them. It was shocking to James because he never saw his parents fight or even argue. His father was rarely home. He grew accustomed to spending time with his mother at church and studying for school. Within a year of the divorce, Robert married his twenty-five-year-old secretary.

James attended the prestigious Fulton Academy in New York City that was named after James Robert Fulton who had been the President of Boston College in the 1870s. Although young James shared the same name as the school's namesake, he was not related to him. This peculiar coincidence made many people at the private high school assume that James was a relative to the famous Catholic priest and dynamic educator of the nineteenth century. A similar assumption was made at Boston College. Since James had an exceptional academic record and was valedictorian of his high school class; he had a great chance of being accepted at the college. However, when the Director of Admissions at Boston College saw the name James Robert Fulton who was graduating from the Fulton Academy and planned on studying theology, he too assumed that James was a relative to the former college president who had also grown up in New York. James Fulton was granted early acceptance and a full scholarship to attend Boston College.

Fulton graduated summa cum laude from Boston College's undergraduate school with degrees in theology and philosophy. He then went on to Boston College Law School graduating summa cum laude. Fulton then graduated from Saint John's Seminary with a master's degree in Theology. He was ordained a Catholic priest and was quickly assigned to the Archdiocese of Boston working directly for Cardinal Harrington. After several years handling administrative duties and successfully resolving important sensitive issues in Boston, he was reassigned to the Archdiocese of New York to clean up similar controversial matters. However, this was not a lateral career move for Fulton. He was appointed to the powerful position of Vicar General and was rumored to be on a fast-track to be elevated to Archbishop. Fulton was both well-liked and feared by people within the Archdiocese because his decisions were final and everyone knew that the Cardinal supported him. That is why everyone in the Archdiocese was shocked when Monsignor Reverend James Robert Fulton, Vicar General of the Archdiocese of New York, suddenly left without discussing his plans with any of his peers or subordinates. If anyone knew the reason, it would be Cardinal Conroy and he was not providing any additional information beyond the official statement that Fulton was on sabbatical.

The airplane was completely full with passengers. In the economy section, several rows from the back of the airplane, Ava sat in the middle seat with earbuds on and was holding an older model iPod. She stared out the window while Fulton was in the aisle seat reading a book. A young woman was asleep with her jacket over her head at the window seat. A middle-aged flight attendant placed a meal box and a bottle of water on the seat-back tray table in front of Ava and did the same for Fulton. Ava removed the earbuds from her ears. Fulton was hungry. He hadn't had anything to eat since early morning. He leaned forward to grab his wrap sandwich from the box then abruptly stopped when he saw Ava make the sign of the cross with her hand moving it to her forehead then to her sternum then to the left shoulder and finally to her right shoulder. She folded her hands, bowed her head, closed her eyes, and prayed silently. Fulton did the same for about a minute. He opened his eyes and looked over to Ava who was smiling at him.

"Are you ready to eat, Monsignor?" Ava asked.

Fulton smiled and thought how he knew why Sister Carmella and the others at the school were so moved by her sweetness. "Yes," Fulton said. "Let's eat."

After finishing their food, Ava picked up her earbuds from her lap.

"You listen to music that I like," Fulton said to her. "I heard Elvis, Bocelli, even some classical music."

"It's my dad's," Ava said motioning to the iPod. "It's his play list. I like listening to it–I think of him."

Fulton smiled and nodded his head and said, "That's nice. Remembering a loved one can be a wonderful vacation for the heart. Are you excited about seeing your aunt?"

"Yes," Ava said.

"Did your mom ever talk about her with you?" Fulton asked.

"Uh-huh. She's in movies. She's an actress," Ava said. "Do you know her?"

"No–I don't," Fulton said with a smile.

"She should be a happy person–she lives in a sunny state," Ava said.

Fulton smiled at her as she pressed the earbuds into her ears. Several moments later the airplane shook violently. Screams and gasps erupted throughout the aircraft cabin as the airplane unexpectedly dropped as if it was being pulled down to the ground. Everyone's eardrums on the airplane popped from the sudden change in altitude. The airplane leveled off then shuttered and then moved as if it was jumping up and down. Fulton's heart pounded in his chest as he tightened his grip on the armrests. He looked over to Ava who appeared very calm while screams from various passengers continued to be heard throughout the cabin. Ava removed her earbuds because she thought Fulton wanted to say something to her.

"Are you okay?" Fulton asked her. Ava nodded her head.

"You're not afraid?" Fulton asked. He was surprised at her calm behavior.

Ava shook her head and said, "We're in God's hands."

The airplane shook violently and descended rapidly again. A bang was heard above. The yellow emergency oxygen masks connected to plastic tubes fell from the ceiling and hung in front of the passengers. Ava bowed her head, closed her eyes, and folded her hands in her lap. Fulton, paralyzed with fright, watched her as she silently prayed in her seat. The plane abruptly stopped shaking and descending to the ground. Fulton was stunned and embarrassed as Ava opened her eyes. The pilot's voice could be heard over the aircraft PA system informing the passengers that they were now out of the area of heavy turbulence and not to be further alarmed. He explained that they had just experienced a strong downward sheer wind that caused the rapid descent, and they were now climbing to a higher altitude. Moments later, the airplane felt as if it was moving upward. The bumpiness ended, and the airplane resumed a steady comfortable flight. Ava looked up at Fulton, smiled, and then put her earbuds back into her ears. Fulton looked back down at his book but could only think about what just happened and wondered if her prayers were actually answered by divine action.

Inside the cockpit, the frightened co-pilot, with his hand still shaking, looked over to the captain for an explanation. "What? You were right here beside me. I don't know what happened. But I'm sticking with what I said to the cabin. A fifteen-thousand-foot drop that quickly! Man–there's no amusement park ride like that! That's the closest to weightlessness those people will ever feel in their lives," the captain said as he reported the incident to the closest traffic control tower. "Denver–this is tango Charlie four-five-one-one calling to report a weather incident."

Fulton and Ava were standing at the counter of a rental car company at the Los Angeles airport. A middle-aged woman was processing their rental transaction. Lewis was positioned out of sight behind a concrete column near a crowd of people standing at the baggage terminal. He watched Fulton and Ava walk toward the rental car parking lot then hurried outside to the curb and hailed a taxi. They got into a beige compact two-door car and drove out of the parking lot. A small yellow taxi minivan, with Lewis inside, followed Fulton and Ava down the road and onto the highway.

It was four o'clock in the afternoon one block away from Venice Beach. The beige compact car drove down the alley behind the glass and stone veneer condo buildings that overlook the beach. A small two-story wooden house was crammed between two six-story sleek modern buildings. The faintest shade of green paint could be seen on the old weathered wood siding of the house. It was as if the house was a large piece of driftwood that washed up from the beach and somehow made its way to this spot behind the oceanfront buildings. There was a rutted gravel driveway between the edge of the alley street and the house.

The beige compact car rolled onto the gravel driveway and stopped in front of the house. A sign read: Tenant Parking Only; it was attached to a steel pole that was in a five-gallon plastic bucket filled with concrete. Fulton and Ava got out of the car. The shade from the surrounding buildings felt good from the hot sun. The tin sound from someone pulling down metal louvers could be heard above them. The shadow of a person could be seen looking down at them from an open second-story window as they walked up the concrete stairs. At the top of the stairs, Fulton looked around for a doorbell to ring.

"What do you want?!" a woman with a raspy smoker's voice yelled down from the other side of the off-white metal louvered blinds.

"We're looking for Desirea Jordan," Fulton said as he stepped back and craned his neck upward attempting to see the person he was speaking with.

"Who's we?!"

"My name's James Fulton, and I'm here with one of Ms. Jordan's relatives," Fulton said.

"My name's Ava," Ava said as she looked up at the second-floor window.

"She's not here! She went to look for work!"

"Oh–do you know when she'll be back?" Fulton asked.

"Argh–enough with the questions already," the woman muttered to herself. "I'm not her DAMN secretary! I don't know when she's coming back! Come back around dinner time! I don't care what you do," the woman yelled as the sound of the metal louvers snapped back into place.

Fulton and Ava looked at each other with uncomfortable expressions. Ava giggled as Fulton motioned for them to go. He looked up to the window and said, "Thank you very much for your time." They walked down the stairs and Fulton said to Ava, "Well, we have some time now, and since we're a block away, we might as well go to the beach and get something to eat." Ava beamed

with joy as she hurried to the car. They hadn't had anything to eat

since they were on the airplane halfway across the country.

Although it was the afternoon on the west coast, their stomachs

were still on east coast time. It was now past dinner back home.

Chapter Three

It was a typical beautiful sunny afternoon in southern California.

Tall palm trees lined the Venice Beach Boardwalk and a concrete

bike path stretched for miles against the white sandy beach.

Among the many t-shirt and trinket shops along the boardwalk was

an old restaurant and bar known as the Beach Café. The restaurant

had a beautiful view of the ocean and a front-row seat to watch the

varied mix of people that went by it. The carnival-like atmosphere

of people along the boardwalk included: inline skaters wearing

bikinis, chain saw jugglers, break-dancers, sidewalk artists, henna

tattoo hawkers, panhandlers, hustlers, musclemen, snake handlers,

religious proselytizers, conga drummers, and mimes.

Ava and Fulton were sitting at a table under the red and white awning of the Beach Café restaurant. A bearded man dressed in a white turban and white robe was playing The Star-Spangled Banner on an electric guitar while slowly moving on inline skates down the boardwalk past the restaurant. Fulton watched the parade of unusual people walk by beyond the restaurant railing while Ava stared at a young lady sitting on the ground between the boardwalk and an adjacent empty paved lot. The young lady was in her early twenties with shoulder-length brown hair. She was wearing a baseball cap and her soiled clothing appeared to have been worn for many days. She sat with her legs crossed and had a sign in front of her that faced the boardwalk.

The waitress, carrying a large tray above her shoulder, came over to their table. She placed a plate down in front of Ava that had a tuna melt sandwich cut into four quarters and a large mound of french fries. A plate of salmon and vegetables was set down in front of Fulton. The waitress walked away from the table as Ava took three quarters of her sandwich and half of her fries and carefully placed them onto her paper napkin that was across her lap. Fulton looked over to Ava expecting that she would want to say a prayer before eating. Instead, Ava said, "Excuse me, Monsignor." She sprang up from her chair cradling the food wrapped in her napkin with both hands and against her stomach. She then ran through the outdoor dining area. Fulton called out to her as she ran past the hostess and out of the restaurant.

Fulton and several of the dining customers watched Ava run over to the young lady sitting with the sign that was leaning against her crossed legs. The sign read: Please help me I'm hungry. The young lady, with a tired dirty face, looked forward with hopeless vacant brown eyes toward the picturesque ocean view. She had sand in her hair and on her clothes from sleeping on the beach at night. Ava knelt down beside her and placed the food wrapped in the napkin on her lap. The young lady was stirred from her trance-like stare toward Ava then down to her lap. It was as if she came back to life. She pulled opened the napkin and grabbed a quarter of the tuna melt sandwich with her dirty fingers. She bit off half of it, chewed a few times then swallowed it as she stuffed the rest of it into her mouth. She looked up to Ava, nodded her head, and mumbled something to her as she continued gorging on the food. The young lady frantically pushed fries into her mouth as she ate the rest of the sandwich trying desperately to extinguish the burning feeling in her stomach that she has had for so long. The initial splitting headache she had from hunger was gone by the third day leaving her in a constant state of being lightheaded, weak, and scared. She couldn't believe that she was eating food again.

Most of the people at the outdoor seating area of the Beach Café were now looking at Ava and the young lady. Various comments were made by the restaurant customers regarding Ava's act of kindness. "Bob, do you see what that little girl is doing? What a sweet girl," one heavy-set woman said that was sitting with her husband near Fulton. The husband responded, "She must be homeless–she was there last night, too."

Two athletically fit men in their thirties were walking along the boardwalk several yards away from Ava. She got up and ran towards them. The diners at the restaurant and some people walking down the boardwalk watched Ava talking to the two men. One of the men handed Ava his unopened plastic bottle of water while the other one removed some money from his fanny pack. He handed a twenty-dollar bill to Ava who then ran back to the young lady on the ground as the two men looked back as they walked away. Ava handed the bottle of water and the twenty-dollar bill to her then pointed to the two men. Ava waved to the two men and they waved back to her. The young lady raised her hand to them with an awkward motion. They waved again as they continued down the boardwalk. Ava said something to the young lady who responded while drinking the water. Ava ran toward the restaurant and stopped before reaching the entrance. She turned back to the young lady and waved good-bye to her. The young lady waved back to her. Ava walked by the hostess who had tears in her eyes and upon entering the outdoor dining area it fell into a hushed silence. Many of the diners had smiles for Ava as she went by and others made complimentary comments. Halfway to her table the restaurant erupted in applause. Ava sat down across from Fulton without saying a word. She reached for the remaining quarter of her sandwich. The hostess came over to Ava and took her plate away and replaced it with another plate that had a new tuna melt sandwich and a huge pile of french fries. "Here you go, honey. You need to eat, too," the hostess said.

"Oh, thank you," Ava said with a big smile.

The hostess bent down toward Ava and said, "Just so you know, every day she's out there–we'll make sure she has food to eat. What you did–was so beautiful." The hostess patted Ava's shoulder and walked away.

"Ava, she's right. That was beautiful–a beautiful act of kindness. You're a very special person. What were you thinking that made you do that?" Fulton said as if he was in a laboratory trying to make sense of an experiment.

Ava finished chewing a mouthful of food. "She looked hungry and sad to me. I had eaten twice already today," she said as she shrugged her shoulders and downplayed what she had done.

"Do you like helping people?" Fulton asked as he went into his familiar role as the prosecutor and judge for all important matters regarding the Archdiocese.

She nodded her head as she pushed a few fries into her mouth and said, "It's what you're supposed to do."

Fulton sat back in his chair and was embarrassed by her response. He was an ordained man of God with a high-level position within the church organization. He was ashamed of himself for walking by this obviously homeless young lady without seeing her and not inviting her to sit down with them to eat. Yet, this eight-year-old saw someone hungry and in need of help. This was another example to him that he was not worthy to serve in his current position at the Archdiocese.

Ava and Fulton finished eating at the restaurant then walked past the Venice Pier on the way back to the rental car. Duval Lewis followed them from a distance while blending in with the crowd of people moving along the boardwalk.

Ava and Fulton walked up the steps of Desirea Jordan's apartment house. Before Fulton was able to ring the doorbell for her apartment; a wet smoker's cough could be heard from the window above them. "She's not back," said the woman from earlier in the day. Fulton stepped back to look up into the window. Ava saw movement at the first-floor window. Someone had pulled the blinds back just enough to see outside.

"Excuse me, what's your name?" Fulton asked.

"What'dya trying to pawn that kid off on me now?" she said.

"Just want to know who I'm speaking with," Fulton said.

"Who are you?"

"I'm James Fulton."

"Yeah–you said that earlier. But who are you? You a cop?"

"No. I'm a Monsignor with the Archdiocese of New York."

"Why aren't you in black? Where's your collar?"

"I'm on vacation."

"What?! I've never heard such a thing! Who's that kid you got with you?! Do you mean to say they let you guys have kids now?!"

"No. Ava is a student at Fontbonne Academy in Manhattan. Ms. Jordan is her great-aunt. We just came by to see her."

Meanwhile, Ava was trying to see who was hiding behind the blinds at the first-floor window. She waved to whoever it was hoping that it would draw them out. The person at the first-floor window stepped away from the blinds.

"Sounds stupid to me; coming all this way from New York! Why didn't you call her before coming?!" she said, followed by a loud cough.

"There was no known number to call Ms. Jordan. Well, I guess we'll come back later."

"Come back?! You sure she doesn't owe you money or something?"

"No. Thank you for your help," Fulton said as he turned away from the window and saw Ava waving toward the first-floor window.

"Cappadonna," the lady from above said then coughed again.

"Excuse me?" Fulton asked as he looked back up to the window.

"My name. You asked me my name. It's Roberta Cappadonna. I'm from Brooklyn."

"Nice to meet you, Roberta. Thank you for your help," Fulton said as he looked away.

"Can you make some prays for me or do I have to go back to church?"

Fulton was surprised by this request and quickly looked back up to the window.

"Monsignor, someone is at the window," Ava whispered to Fulton.

"Wait one minute, please," Fulton said as he briefly looked back to Ava then returned his eyes to the window above him.

"What'dya saying?!" Roberta asked.

"I will pray for you. What would you like me to pray for?"

"Oh boy–it's like to talking to a genie and having only one wish. He knows what I need. Just get him to take care of me."

"Very well. May God Almighty hear your prayers and have mercy on you. Amen."

"Amen. Thank you, Monsignor. Desirea! You have visitors! Open your door!" Roberta yelled out the window.

Fulton looked over to Ava then to the first-floor window. The blinds moved again. Footsteps could be heard coming to the front door. The door opened and a thin woman in her late sixties, wearing make-up and dressed to appear younger, stepped forward in the doorway.

"Thanks a lot, Roberta!" Desirea yelled as she looked upward.

"I tried to get rid them for you. But when I found out who he works for–I wasn't messing with him. I've got enough problems!" Roberta said.

Desirea turned to Ava and Fulton who were standing on the landing at the top of the stairs.

"Aunt Desirea–I'm Ava. I'm so happy to meet you," Ava said as she stepped forward and hugged Desirea around her waist who immediately stiffened up then awkwardly patted her on the shoulder.

"Yeah–nice to meet you. You're Margie's kid, right?" Desirea said trying to be social.

"Uh-huh," Ava said as she nodded with a big smile and looked up at her.

"I guess you are–you've got her smile and everything," Desirea said then looked over to Fulton. "You're Monsignor…"

"James Fulton. It's pleasure to meet you–Ms. Jordan," Fulton said as he extended his hand to her. Desirea raised her hand to his and quickly shook it.

"Yep. Come on inside so we can at least have some privacy," Desirea said as she stepped back from the doorway. Fulton and Ava followed her inside.

A few feet inside the modestly furnished apartment, Fulton saw framed pictures of Desirea with various celebrities spanning several decades on the wall and on a bookshelf.

"I see you're in the entertainment business," Fulton said while scanning the pictures of movie and television stars from the 1960s to the 1990s.

"I used to think so. Not so sure of that now. Bit parts turned into doing extra work," Desirea said as she tightened her mouth.

"My mother said she's a movie star in Hollywood," Ava said to Fulton. Desirea laughed. At that moment a hairy blur moved quickly across the carpet. Ava was greeted by a small silver-blue and pale cream dog that ran from a back room yapping away.

"Oh, it's a Yorkshire terrier! It's so cute!" Ava exclaimed as she dropped down to her knees. The dog let out a deep bark.

"Bruno," Desirea said to calm him down. Bruno ran over to Ava and began licking her hand. "Be a good boy."

"Bruno–you're so cute," Ava said as she giggled from Bruno climbing up on her legs.

"Ava–you stay here and play with Bruno. You can watch TV. I'm going take the Monsignor in the kitchen for some tea," Desirea said as she turned on the TV before walking into the kitchen.

Bruno barked and yelped as he ran around Ava making her laugh as she tried to pet him. Fulton followed Desirea into the kitchen.

"What's going on? Something wrong with the kid's mother?" Desirea asked as she took a position by the stove and folded her arms in front of herself.

"I'm afraid so. She has inoperable brain cancer," Fulton said.

"Oh, that's horrible. That poor kid can't get a break. Her father was killed in Iraq just a few years ago, right?" Desirea said as she tried to remember when she got the letter from her niece.

"Sister Carmella–she's the principal at Fontbonne Academy where Ava attends school; she told me that he died four years ago. Ms. Jordan–the reason we're out here…" Fulton said.

"I'm no mother. I can't raise that kid," Desirea said sternly as she shook her head. "I'm too old and wouldn't know what to do."

"Well, it's hasn't come to that yet. As I understand, you're the only living relative. Ava's mother had listed you as the next of kin in case of an emergency."

"Yeah–without my say so. I would think that she needs my permission," Desirea said as her hand trembled.

"Ms. Jordan, don't concern yourself with that. Sister Carmella said that she can provide parental oversight and safety for Ava should her mother pass."

"You said it was brain cancer, right? The only outcome is that. What'dya mean safety and parental guidance from this Sister

Carmine or whatever her name is? What does she want with the girl?"

"The Division of Child Services came to the school this morning and was trying to take custody of Ava. Sister Carmella offered to let Ava stay at the school on the residence floor for the nuns while her mother was in the hospital. The city official rejected that offer and is determined to take custody of Ava and place her in a foster home. Sister Carmella asked me to accompany Ava out here to meet you, and to get an understanding from you, in the event that her mother passes away, what is the best possible outcome for her."

"Oh, I see–you took the kid and ran out of Dodge before they grabbed her. Huh, I didn't think NUNS would do that. And look– she's got a Monsignor as an escort. The kid's doing pretty good. Like I was saying, I can't take this kid in. But I know some of those foster kids get abused and then I don't want her to be stuck in a convent her whole life either!"

"Providing that her mother doesn't have a will that directs custody to someone other than you–Ava could stay at the school to complete her education at no expense to you and you could retain custody over her and we could even arrange it so you receive a regular stipend from the school for any costs that she may create for you."

Desirea stared at Fulton with a suspicious glare. "Why does the school want to help her so much and even pay me off?! What's going on?!"

"Your niece's daughter is a special girl. Sister Carmella and the other nuns have developed a close bond with her as have her classmates. This desire to assist Ava is purely of good intentions and what is best for the child. You're welcome to travel to visit the school and meet with Sister Carmella. Of course, we would cover all of your expenses."

"Do you work at the school?"

"No. I work at the Archdiocese in Midtown Manhattan."

"So, why didn't Sister Chiquita come out here instead of you? A monsignor trumps a nun!"

"I'm on sabbatical–coincidently, I was visiting the school today when child services showed up. I attended Fontbonne and was one of Sister Carmella's students. She couldn't leave the school and she asked me to take Ava out here and meet with you. That's it."

"How much of a stipend?"

"We'll make sure that it's fair and acceptable to you."

"I'm not sure about this. I'm gonna have to think about it. Anyway–we better get out there. It's awful quiet. Let's see what she and that dog are up to."

Fulton and Desirea left the kitchen and walked into the front room. Ava was asleep on the couch cradling Bruno like a baby in her lap. Bruno opened his eyes to see who was there then shut them closed. Fulton looked over to Desirea who smiled for the first time as she looked at Ava and Bruno on the couch. A clock read: 7:00 PM.

"Ms. Jordan, why don't you let Ava sleep here tonight? I'll stay at the hotel down the street and will come back in the morning for her."

A shocked look appeared on Desirea's face. "What?"

"I promise–I'll be back tomorrow morning. It's really late for her. She's exhausted. She won't be any trouble for you."

"All right–since you're coming back tomorrow morning."

Fulton saw a framed picture of a young girl on a shelf. He walked toward it, picked it up, and examined it. "This girl looks like Ava," Fulton said.

"It's her mother. She came out to stay with me a few times when she was young. She then came out after she got married, and I met her husband who was in the Army."

"It's incredible! They look exactly alike."

Fulton left Desirea's house and drove down the street to the hotel located a few blocks away. Lewis was in the backseat of a taxi talking to someone on his cellphone as he watched Fulton enter the hotel.

"Something big is going on. A guy in his position doesn't escort a kid across the country. I'm staying on this–I'll be sleeping in the hotel lobby tonight. When this story breaks–you and I will be talking about a big pay raise and my own column," Lewis said into the telephone as he handed his credit card to the taxi driver.

Chapter Four

It was 2:00 AM at the Venice Fishing Pier. The 1,310-foot-long concrete structure juts out into the ocean like a long bony finger with a 120-foot diameter circular platform at the end of it. People fish off the pier during the day and a small odd group of hard-core regulars come in the evening when it is closed. The strong briny smell of the ocean was interrupted by the hot, dry Santa Ana winds blowing westward off the mountains and onto the water. Ocean waves, two to three feet high, rolled under the pier and collapsed onto the beach. This particular evening millions of stars embedded across the night sky sparkled bright above the dark ocean.

Three men, well-fit, in their mid-thirties, each holding two fishing poles, were positioned along the railing at the very end of the pier. Jim Thomas and Pedro Garcia did three tours of military duty in Iraq and remained extremely close after their service together. Their war experience continued to impact them years later; so much so that instead of tossing and turning trying to sleep at night, they would go fishing every evening. Juan, Pedro's younger brother by one year, served two tours of combat duty in Afghanistan.

Nearby, two other men, both heavy set with beards consisting of several days of growth, each holding a bottle of wine, were sitting on the ground leaning against railing posts. One of the two, Pablo, passed out from drinking too much. An empty wine bottle slipped from his grasp and rolled away hitting another empty bottle. The other drinker pushed and shook Pablo's shoulder attempting to wake him up while offering some of his wine.

"Tito—ALTO! Leave him alone! He's had enough," Juan yelled as he held onto two fishing poles by the railing.

"He wants more. Mas vino amigo?" Tito said as he continued to nudge the semi-conscious man who mumbled something to him.

Juan was holding two fishing poles as he moved along the railing toward Tito. Juan kicked Tito's shoulder.

"No more wine for him!" Juan growled to Tito as Pablo was emerging from his drunken stupor and attempted to sit-up. "If I have to put my poles down–I'm throwing you over the rail," Juan said to Tito.

"Okay–take it easy. I was just…trying to help my best friend– Pablo Perez. Right Pablo–Perez? He's got a nice name, huh?" Tito said as he took another swig of wine.

"Hey, Pablo–no more wine. Lay down–go to sleep," Juan said to Pablo who slowly laid down and went to sleep.

"Juan, you should be like your brother. You're not in the army no more," Tito said. "Don't give orders!"

"Tito–shut up before I THROW you over the rail!" Pedro said as he continued facing the ocean while chewing on a plastic straw.

"I say we throw him over anyways. Like my grandfather used to say–get rid of anything bad as soon as you can–it'll only get worse," Jim said as he leaned on the railing while holding two fishing poles. Jim was tall and walked with a limp. He kept his hair long enough to hide the missing top half of his left ear. His injuries were from a roadside bomb explosion in Iraq.

"No, Jimmy–he'll stink up the water so bad; the fish will crawl onto the beach. We'll never catch anything out here," Pedro said.

Jim and Juan laughed. A few seconds later, the fishing rod in Pedro's right hand jerked forward then bent downward. Pedro immediately stood up and pulled the rod upward. "Whoa!" Pedro exclaimed.

Jim and Juan moved over towards Pedro. Jim slammed one of his fishing poles into a hole along the railing then grabbed the other fishing pole from Pedro's left hand. Pedro cranked the handle winding the fishing line in. He continued to work the pole up then cranked the line in. "All right, Pedro! Pulled in! Don't lose him!" Jim said.

The pole bent down and pulled Pedro to the rail. Juan grabbed Pedro by the belt and pulled him upright as he held his two fishing poles in his right hand.

"It's frigg'in big!" Juan yelled as he stood back up from the rail.

Pedro struggled with the pole as it bent down toward the ocean pulling him onto the rail again. Jim dropped the two fishing poles and put his arms around Pedro's waist. Juan did the same and held onto Pedro's belt with both hands. The fishing pole snapped in half and then was ripped from Pedro's hands. All three men fell backwards onto the concrete platform.

"You think it was SHARK?!" Juan yelled.

"It was BIG," Pedro said, exhausted and rattled.

"Bigger than a SHARK?!" Juan exclaimed.

"Tomorrow at work–it'll be a <u>whale</u>, right Pedro?" Jim said then imitated Juan. "Last night, my brother, Pedro–he hooked frigg'in Shamu!"

The three men laughed as they scrambled to get the fishing poles still lying on the ground. As they maneuvered the fishing poles between them and passed a few back and forth to untangle the lines Juan looked out over the ocean.

"Hey, do you guys see that?!" Juan exclaimed as he pointed straight out at the night sky over the ocean. "It's a shooting star! See it crossing the sky! What the?!"

Jim and Pedro looked up from their fishing poles.

"You mean right there?" Jim said pointing lower to a bright light that looked like a bright star on the horizon above the ocean. "That's a ship or maybe a plane."

"That's not a ship. It's moving too fast. It's probably a navy jet," Pedro said.

"I saw it shoot across the sky, then it stopped in midair, and then it went straight down really fast–jets don't move like that," Juan said trying to make sense of what he saw.

The bright light appeared to being moving toward them as the horizon lit up with glowing orange and red color that spread across the sky. The bright light grew larger as it continued to move towards them.

"It's the SUN! It's rising–like it does every morn'in," Tito said slurring his words as he looked through his bloodshot eyes over his shoulder toward the ocean.

"That's not the sun," Jim and Pedro said together.

"It rises back THERE–over the mountains and not for another four hours," Pedro said as he motioned over his shoulder with his thumb.

The star-like light grew brighter and larger as it moved toward them.

"It's coming right at US," Jim stated with growing concern.

They stepped back a few feet from the railing as the star-like light expanded instantly to the width of the horizon making the night into daytime. The searing brightness blinded them as they felt a surge of incredible heat as if they were standing by an open furnace. This was followed by a powerful hot wind off the ocean that pushed them back a few feet. An unexpected shockwave passed over them knocking them backwards to the ground. They all groaned from the impact.

"Pedro–I can't see!" Juan cried out to his brother as he blinked his eyes.

They were all blinded by the sudden intensity of the light. After blinking several times, they looked up and saw a man standing on the railing. He had a closely trimmed beard and was wearing a blazing white robe, a blazing white keffiyeh wrapped around his head, and leather sandals. The daylight dimmed back to nighttime except for an incredible white-golden aura around the man on the railing. The pain each one of them was feeling was eliminated as soon as he looked at them. They sat speechless as he moved from the top of the railing down onto the surface of the pier within the blink of an eye. He stood for a moment in front of them then walked past them. He continued walking away from the end of the pier and went past Tito and Pablo who were still laying on the ground.

Pablo watched the man dressed in the white robe as he walked off the circular end of the pier onto the long narrow stretch that led to the shore. Tito looked down at his bottle of wine and let it roll away from him. Thwack. A twenty-inch-long fish dripping with water hit the ground of the pier between Jim and Pedro. This was followed with several more fish hitting the ground then hundreds of fish poured onto the pier as if they were being sucked up from the ocean by an industrial vacuum. Jim, Pedro, and Juan scrambled to their feet, but fell down from the ever-increasing number of fish coming onto the pier. They slipped and stumbled as they tried to get up again. Crawling on the ground over the flipping and flopping fish towards Pablo and Tito; they kept moving across the pier away from the railing. Thousands of fish continued to pour onto the pier at the spot where the man in the white robe had stood, piling up onto each other, floundering about against each other, and spreading out across the entire circular end of the concrete structure.

About halfway down the pier a white light raced down from the night sky and hit the ground several feet in front of the man in the white robe. The beam of light on the ground changed into a human-like form wearing a golden robe that was kneeling on one knee. His head was looking down and in his right hand he held a large sword of shimmering light. The man in the white robe stood above the person on one knee.

"My Lord–you summoned me," the person said without raising his head.

"Michael."

"Yes–my Lord. The twelve legions are ready for you. Is it today–my Lord?" Michael said.

"Stand ready. But, do not take action until I command thee."

"Yes–my Lord," Michael replied.

The man in the white robe continued walking down the pier then disappeared into the darkness before reaching the shore. Michael stood up and looked at the shore and then towards the mountains. Another person that was slightly taller appeared near Michael. He was dressed in a beautifully tailored dark-gray suit and black leather shoes. He was a handsome man with black hair and a trim athletic build.

"What is he doing here?!" said the man in the dark-gray suit.

"He will go wherever he wants to," Michael said.

"He is not expected to be coming back here now, is he?! What's the meaning of this?!"

"Only he and his father know the precise moment of the judgement," Michael said.

"I would be aware of it! This is my domain!"

"You are a temporary steward serving a purpose here," Michael said.

"What are you here for then?!"

"I remain at the ready for him," Michael responded.

"You're a hypocrite! You're no different than me! Look—you're never without the sword! Your whole purpose is to destroy!"

"I am an instrument created by God Almighty to be used against you and your evil entanglements. You have created quite a mess here: killing, pain, and suffering through war. And still more suffering through poverty, adultery, lying and stealing. You have humans hating each other over the color of their skin or the location of their birth. And most recently, you have created a never-ending spiral of self-worship. The judgement here–it's long overdue," Michael said.

"You're a FOOL! I was created by him before this Son of Man was! I am part of his divine human game he created! I am the principle part of the test for these worthless creatures that continue to disappoint him! He needs me so he can sort out the chaff! If you ask ME, they're all–no good! He would have had better results with the monkeys and apes!"

It was 2:10 AM in Compton, California. Five young men, in their early to mid-twenties, tough looking from life-on the-street living, were standing on the corner of Royall and Green Street under a dimly lit street light. They were in their neighborhood yet that didn't stop them from continually looking around and staying vigilant. Two nights prior, a rival gang had surprised them with a drive-by shooting in attempt to expand territory. Several bullets zipped by them at the same location. It was important for them to show that they were not afraid, and that they owned the neighborhood. A police siren could be heard going by one block away which triggered dogs barking throughout the neighborhood.

"Damn dogs–barking! Sirens going every five minutes here! What they barking for?!" Ty said as he shook his head.

"Shoot–I thought that bark'in was your girl calling you home," Blue said then spit on the ground as the rest of the gang laughed.

"Shut your face, Blue! At least I got a girl. Your sister don't count," Ty said.

"Ooooo!" TK, Grill, and GI Joe exclaimed.

"Who's got the skills?!" TK yelled.

"What's going on?! Is this play time?!" Teddy Webster exclaimed as he approached them.

Teddy was thirty years old, six feet-four inches tall, and had a muscular large frame that was covered in scars from gunshots, stabbings, and fights. He was a fearless man with a widespread reputation of someone you don't want to cross. His infamous street battles and hospital visits have earned him great respect from larger rival gangs.

"Teddy–we're just here–watch'in the street," Ty said as the five men straightened up and spread out a few feet farther from each other.

"You gotta watch it. You lose the street–the neighborhood's gone," Teddy said as he looked at each of the five men taking a moment to stare into their eyes. "We good?! It's our street– nobody's gonna take it!"

All of the men affirmed their commitment to the neighborhood as a person dressed in dark clothing could be seen walking down the street toward them. Ty motioned with his head and jutting his jaw forward to the stranger's location.

"Who's this?!" Ty said. "Hey!" he yelled to the stranger.

They all watched the stranger turn into an alley.

"He's runn'in down the ALLEY?!" Ty said.

"Dumbass needs some GPS," Blue said.

"He needs to learn not to come around here! Go give it to him–NOW!" Teddy said.

The five men grabbed metal pipes that were stashed around them for protection. Ty was holding a five-foot-high steel pry bar in his hands as he nodded his head to Teddy. Blue and Ty ran across the street and went into the trash strewn alley. Teddy, TK, Grill, and GI Joe walked across the street, stopped at the entrance of the alley, and looked around to make sure it wasn't a trap that was set-up by a rival gang. Teddy looked down the dark alley but couldn't see anything.

Ty and Blue stopped running a few yards away from the stranger who was facing the ten-foot-high rusted steel gate at the end of the alley. He wasn't trying to scale the chain-link fencing on the gate to get away, nor seemed to be concerned with the current situation.

"Maybe he's got a gun," Ty said.

"We'll find out," Blue said as he motioned with his metal pipe.

"Yeah," Ty said as he raised the long steel pry bar upward and moved towards the stranger.

Meanwhile, Teddy, TK, Grill, and GI Joe were standing at the end of the alley watching the street. There was a flash of light behind them. Teddy and the other gang members turned back toward the alley.

"What was that, Teddy?!" TK exclaimed.

A moment later, something landed on the ground with a loud clang in front of Teddy and the others. It was the five-foot-long steel pry bar that Ty was carrying which was now twisted up and around like a giant pretzel.

"What the hell?! Teddy–what the HELL?!" TK yelled with uncontrollable fear. "He's freak'in superman!"

"Bullshit," Teddy said as he pulled a 9mm semi-automatic handgun from inside his jacket. "We'll see if superman is faster than a bullet. Come on."

Teddy led the way down the alley followed by TK, Grill, and GI Joe who were holding their metal pipes up high as if they were ready to swing at a pitched ball. They got down to the end of the alley. The stranger was several yards away still facing the steel gate. Between them and the stranger, there were two large lumps on the ground. Teddy held his handgun with both hands aiming at the back of the stranger.

"What's that on the ground?" TK asked standing near Teddy.

"Go see if it's Ty and Blue–you damn fool!" Teddy yelled as he kept aim at the back of the stranger.

TK nervously stepped forward still holding his metal pipe up high ready to swing at the stranger or anybody else. He kicked the lump closest to him then did the same to the next one.

"Clothes!" TK yelled visibly frightened. "It's just clothes!"

"What?!" Teddy said.

"Clothes! You know–pants, jacket! What we wear!" TK shrieked as he stepped back to Teddy, Grill, and GI Joe.

"Are they TY's and Blue's?!" Teddy asked.

"I don't know!" TK exclaimed. "They look like their shoes!"

"Where are they?!" Teddy asked the stranger facing the steel gate. "I said–where are they?!"

There was no response from the stranger still facing the steel gate. Teddy fired seven shots from his handgun into the back of the stranger. Only TK, Grill, and GI Joe moved from the ear-piercing rapid sound of the gunfire. The spent brass shell casings pinged against the old worn asphalt. The stranger continued to face the steel gate. Fear appeared on Teddy's face as he kept the handgun aimed at the stranger. He knew he didn't miss him. He was sure that he fired directly at his back.

"Shoot him again, Teddy! Shoot HIM!" TK and GI Joe yelled.

Teddy braced himself and squeezed the trigger. Nothing happened. He squeezed it again. Nothing happened. Teddy checked the handgun. There was a bullet in the chamber. He took aim at the stranger.

"Shoot HIM! Shoot HIM!" TK, Grill, and GI Joe yelled.

Teddy squeezed the trigger several more times. Nothing happened. The stranger slowly turned around, and before they could see his face in the shadows, an intense bright white light came out from him. The beam of light hit TK, Grill, and GI Joe instantly vaporizing them where they stood leaving only a pile of clothes on the ground. Teddy quickly looked down and saw that TK, Grill, and GI Joe were gone. He was paralyzed in fear as he stood there. He was then unexpectedly thrown backwards to the pavement and writhed about from excruciating pain that he felt throughout his body. After several moments, the pain stopped. Teddy laid dazed and motionless on the ground. He looked up and saw the stranger standing by the steel gate. There was a bright light illuminating from within the man yet Teddy could not see his face. But he did hear a familiar voice that said, "Teddy."

Teddy sat up and looked at what appeared to be movement behind the stranger. An elderly, black women dressed in a blue and white print Sunday dress, wearing a small blue box hat with a white veil and white cotton gloves, stepped from behind the stranger.

"Theodore Lincoln Webster–you ought to be ashamed of yourself!" the elderly woman exclaimed as she bent slightly forward, raised her hand and pointed her finger at him.

"Huh? It can't be," Teddy said as he shook his head trying to see if he was dreaming.

"Teddy, your grandpa and me raised you to be a GOOD–God fearing young man! You promised me–you promised me that you would live a Christian life and be one of the Lord's soldiers," she said as she stepped towards Teddy.

"Gram? It can't be you. You're dead," Teddy said shaking his head in disbelief.

"Teddy, how could you do all of those terrible things and throw your living soul away forever?! What were you thinking?! Don't you remember what I taught you?! What I told you?! God sees everything."

"What's happening?! I must be dead?!" Teddy said.

"No Teddy, you're alive–unlike your friends."

"Where are they, Gram?"

"They're gone."

"But their clothes are here. Why are the clothes here?"

"Oh, my sweet boy, they don't need clothes where they've gone to."

"What's going to happen to me, Gram?"

"You've been given another chance."

"Another chance? Another chance for what, Gram?"

She smiles for the first time and said, "He has a plan for you. I'm so happy for you." She then vanished as the stranger stepped forward. Teddy's eyes grew wide with astonishment

Chapter Five

Later that morning sirens blared from the street below. Fulton

rolled over in his bed and looked at the clock which read: 5:45

AM. Fulton was still on east coast time and had been awake for the

past three hours. He got out of bed, went to the window, and pulled

back the orange-yellow stripe pattern drapes. The view from his

room looked out to the ocean and to the far left was the Venice

Pier. He saw police cars and emergency response vehicles parked

at the entrance of the pier. Fulton thought that they must be

responding to someone that had been engaged in some type of

illicit behavior on the pier. He reached for the remote and turned

on the television. The television screen lit up with the image of a newscaster reporting on a motor vehicle accident then it changed to a flickering snowy picture before turning black. Fulton shut off the television and turned it back on. The screen was black for a moment then three words appeared on it that read: I am Here.

Fulton was startled. He stepped back and stared at the television screen. He initially thought he was going crazy or someone was playing a joke on him. But he quickly dismissed those possibilities when he thought about what had happened to the television screen back in the guest room at Fontbonne Academy and the strange event yesterday on the airplane. The telephone on the nightstand rang. Fulton picked up the telephone as the message on the television screen disappeared. It was Sister Carmella on the telephone.

"They know that you took her to Los Angeles," Sister Carmella said.

"Who does?" Fulton asked.

"Child services. They've filed a motion to take custody of Ava and are requesting assistance from the City of Los Angeles to hold her in protective custody until they can send someone out to get her," Sister Carmella said.

Fulton told Sister Carmella about his conversation with Desirea Jordan and that he thought that she would agree to some type of co-guardianship role providing she visited the school. Sister Carmella did not want to risk Ava being in anyone's custody but Ava's own mother or someone at the school. She requested that Fulton take Ava out of Los Angeles immediately. He hesitated until he looked over to the television screen and read the following: Get Ava Go Now. Fulton assured Sister Carmella that he would take Ava out of Los Angeles and keep her at a safe location.

Meanwhile, down at the Venice Pier, emergency responders waded through a knee-high layer of struggling fish that covered the circular end of the pier. Firemen used shovels and other tools to push the fish off the pier and into the water. As the wind blew eastward, the smell of fish mixed with the refreshing scent of the ocean. A drone flew in a circle over the scene. Two uniformed policemen and a fire captain stood on the pier away from the fish that were floundering about. The younger policeman checked his shoes and pants for any unwanted stains from the fish.

"Who owns that?" Fire Captain Farrington asked as he pointed to the drone flying above them.

"Probably the media. They're down at the gate waiting for a statement," Police Sergeant Dryden said.

"Do we know how these fish got up here? Did anyone see anything?" Fire Captain Farrington asked.

"There were some local guys that are regulars out here. They said there was a bright light, some guy appeared on the railing, floated down to the ground, and then walked away from them.

Then they said the fish came out of the water," Police Sergeant Dryden said.

"Were they drunk or on drugs?" Fire Captain Farrington asked.

"They admitted to drinking–a few beers each," the younger policeman said as he looked down to the small narrow notepad in his hand for the information.

"Is there anything else?" Fire Captain Farrington asked.

"The state environmental guy said it could have been caused by a rogue wave or solar flares disrupting the magnetic field around the earth," Police Sergeant Dryden said then rolled his eyes.

"What?! Was he drinking with the guys fishing?!" Fire Captain Farrington said.

"That's what we said. Then he said to us–it was because of global warming," Police Sergeant Dryden said flipping his notepad closed.

"Really–GLOBAL WARMING?! Ah, what the heck–I'll go with that," Fire Captain Farrington said as he shrugged his shoulders, turned away from the policemen, and walked toward the shore to meet with the press. The drone buzzed around overhead as the emergency personnel continued to push thousands of fish off the pier.

Later that morning, Fulton and Ava were in the rental car driving down the highway. Ava was eating a blueberry muffin and drinking orange juice from a small paper carton.

"Where are we going?" Ava asked.

"To Las Vegas–to see a friend of mine," Fulton said.

"What's his name?" Ava asked.

"Arturo Benez," Fulton said.

"Does he live in a church?"

"Yes, in the back of it. He's a church bishop."

"Did you stay in a church last night?"

"No–in a hotel," he chuckled.

Ava was quiet for a few moments. "Are you still on vacation?" she asked.

"Ah, yes. I am. Why do ask?"

"Does that mean I'm on vacation?"

"Yeah–you are, too," Fulton said with a smile. "We need to make sure you have some fun."

"It feels like I'm on vacation," Ava said. "After we see your friend, are we going back to see Aunt Desirea?"

"I don't think so. We'll probably just fly back home."

"Do you know my mom?"

"No–I'm sorry that I don't. Sister Carmella has told me all about her."

"Is Sister Carmella your mother?"

"No. She was my teacher when I was a student at Fontbonne."

"When we get back home, do you want to meet my mom?"

"Yes, I would very much like to."

Fulton and Ava drove along on the highway. Ava had her earbuds on and was listening to music that was loud enough that Fulton could hear it as well. He was enjoying her dad's playlist tapping his fingers on the steering wheel to an old Elvis Presley song that Ava was often humming or singing on the trip. Fulton looked up at the rearview mirror and saw a car hanging back from them. He got a strange feeling. He switched lanes and watched the car move into the same lane. Fulton was driving the speed limit and become suspicious of the car behind them. He noticed an exit ramp for gas service and food one hundred yards ahead. At the last possible moment, he turned sharply onto the ramp without using his turn signal. The tires squealed as the car lurched to the right and Ava's small frame shifted to the left in her seat. The car behind them did the same maneuver. Fulton drove through the parking lot winding around groups of cars and trucks. He pulled the car into a parking spot and turned around to see who was driving the car that was following them. It was the reporter–Duval Lewis. Fulton realized that Lewis followed them out to Los Angeles and probably informed the Division of Child Services of Ava's whereabouts. He knew he had to somehow getaway from Lewis and prevent him from following them to Las Vegas. Fulton tapped a few icons on the dashboard screen for the GPS system that was in the rental car.

"Since we're officially on vacation–how would you like to visit a national park?" Fulton asked Ava.

Meanwhile, Lewis sat in his rental car that he picked up at the hotel. He was talking with someone on his cell phone while watching Fulton and Ava who were still in their car.

"They're parked a few rows over from me after turning on two wheels into this rest stop. I thought he spotted me and was trying to get away, but I think he just saw the exit ramp late. I don't know what he's doing–we're driving towards Vegas. You know, I was thinking, maybe this kid–is HIS. Imagine that. That's gotta be a Pulitzer for me, right? Maybe we run with that regardless if it's true. Oh, wait–they're getting out of the car. I'll call you back," Lewis said as he watched Fulton and Ava walk toward the restrooms.

Lewis, wearing sunglasses, put a baseball cap on his head while he waited until they went into the building then he followed them in. He entered the men's room and ducked into the first empty stall. After a few minutes, he peered through the space between the door and the stall frame to see Fulton washing his hands at the sink. Lewis silently counted to ten before leaving the stall and exiting the men's room. He looked down with his sunglasses on trying to hide his face when he glanced over and saw Fulton and Ava inside the convenient store picking out snacks and some drinks. Lewis quickly slipped down the first aisle. He grabbed a few food items and stuffed them into his jacket pockets. Lewis then walked over to the soda fountain machine. He filled a large paper cup with soda and then began drinking it as he walked over to the magazine display area. He carefully positioned himself to keep an eye on Fulton and Ava. After Fulton paid for their items, they both left the store. Lewis took one last gulp of his soda, then left it on a shelf by the magazines, and walked out of the store without paying for anything. Outside the rest area building, Fulton and Ava got into their car and drove onto the highway with Lewis close behind them.

After driving for an hour on the highway, Fulton and Ava took the exit for the Wilderness National Park. They drove down the main road with Lewis following them from a distance. Fulton thought that in order for them to lose Lewis before getting to Las Vegas, he would have to take advantage of any opportunity that arises in this expansive forest park. They sped along the main park road past some people in a vintage, shiny metallic Airstream camper that had pulled off the road. Scrub brush, barrel cactus, and cholla cactus were scattered across the vast open space on both sides of the road with the Wilderness Mountains in front of them out in the distance.

"Are we going camping?" Ava asked.

"No. We're just passing through and enjoying the sights," Fulton said as he kept an eye on the rearview mirror.

They stopped at the park entrance and took a map from the park ranger who was sitting on a wooden chair in a sun-aged wooden gatehouse. The park ranger was in his early sixties and was dressed in a green uniform. He advised them to keep to the posted speed limit because of the unpredictability of the wildlife and park visitors. The park ranger also warned them about the fluctuation in temperature because the park has a cooler forest wilderness in the mountains and warmer high and low desert climates in other areas. They drove down the main road with Lewis' car always behind them in the distance.

Fulton took the mountain road that led to the forest wilderness instead of the road that went to the desert. He thought that the forest would provide the best chance to get away from Lewis. Fulton maintained a conversation with Ava as they enjoyed the magnificent towering spruce and pine trees that increased in density as the road switched back and forth as they traveled upward. He opened the two front windows and told Ava to take a deep breath and smell the fresh fragrant air. Ava kept inhaling as if she was going to hold her breath for a period of time. She marveled at the scent and said that each breath she took felt like she was cleaning her lungs.

Fulton looked at the park road map depicted on the car's GPS navigation screen. He was hoping for a road intersection or some other opportunity to lose Lewis in the park. Fulton was frustrated because he knew that it would be difficult to lose him since Lewis was driving further back, and he would always have enough time to change course to follow them. Ava glanced over to Fulton then back to looking at the scenic view through the windshield.

"Whenever something's bothering you, or you need help, all you have to do is just pray," Ava said as she continued looking at the stunning view as they climbed higher into the mountains.

Fulton immediately thought about their flight when the plane was violently shaking and how it appeared to have stopped from her prayers being answered. "Will you pray with me?" Fulton asked Ava.

"Yes, but please don't close your eyes while you're driving," Ava said as she shut her eyes and folded her hands in her lap.

Fulton prayed for something to happen on the park road so that they could get away from Lewis. It was a quick prayer. Fulton took his eyes off the road and quickly looked over to Ava who then opened her eyes. They drove by a thick growth of low hanging spruce trees. Something emerged from the shadows on the passenger side of the car. It was so large and close to them. Fulton, from his peripheral vision, was sure that it was going to broadside them. He swerved to the left side of the road to avoid the impending impact. A large family RV emerged from the low arching evergreen branches and then moved onto the road. A loud horn blared ahead of them followed by the sound of screeching tires. Fulton, who had been looking up at the rearview mirror, looked forward through the windshield and saw another large RV heading down the road. The RV that rushed out of the forest had come to a full stop across the pavement blocking the road. The second RV had black smoke coming from its tires as the large vehicle shuddered on the pavement as it swerved to the right then stopped off the road. Fulton gasped as he expected to hear the dreaded sound of metal hitting metal from a crash. There was no crash. Fulton pulled the car over to the right, stopping it on the shoulder of the road, and told Ava to stay put. He got of the car and ran back to the RVs. A middle-aged man got out of the second RV while two other older men got out of the first RV. They all said to Fulton that they were not injured as other people from the RVs disembarked to inspect for any damage. One of the RV passengers was already calling the park emergency number for assistance. The driver of the first RV couldn't start the engine and the second RV had a flat tire from driving onto sharp pointed rocks when it went off the road. Fulton asked again if they needed any help which they declined as they became fully engaged in a conversation on how the accident happened. Fulton spotted Lewis coming from behind the first RV striking up a conversation with a middle-aged woman. Fulton stepped away from the people milling about the disabled vehicles and quickly walked to his car. He hopped into the driver's seat and slowly drove away from the scene.

"Is everyone okay?" Ava asked as she was kneeling in her seat looking at the accident scene through the rear window.

"Miraculously–everyone is fine," Fulton answered as he looked up at the rearview mirror and saw Lewis frantically trying to get one of the RVs to move so he could get around them in his car.

As soon as they were out of sight, Fulton increased the speed of the car. He knew that they only had a little time before Lewis would get by the RVs and be back to following them. They drove by a gravel road that led to a campground. Fulton thought that if he stayed on the main road, Lewis would eventually catch up to them. He decided that he would pull over somewhere out of sight and let Lewis drive past them. They would then go back onto the main road and drive out the way they came into the park. A road sign ahead of them read: Old Sawmill Road. Fulton turned onto the rutted gravel road. The road was lined with mature trees with massive branches that were interlocked high above it. This connected tree canopy was so dense that it dimmed the light from the noontime sun and simulated a natural tunnel as they drove along. After driving for a half-hour, the road ended at an old abandoned sawmill. They drove by two smaller log cabin-style buildings with roofs that had long collapsed exposing the inside to the weather. The car stopped in front of a large, dark wooden building that stood one and half stories high and could have easily accommodated a cut log over a hundred feet long. Fulton and Ava got out of the car by the end of the building and could hear the sound of rushing water. There was a thick wooden door that was slightly ajar at that end of the building. There was a lone window near the door with only a tattered canvas tarp barely hanging across it. As Ava walked by the window something unexpectedly came out from behind the tarp and brushed against her hair and forehead. Ava jumped back as a barn swallow flew past her and disappeared into the woods.

"Oh, my GOSH! That scared me," Ava exclaimed as she put her hand to her chest.

"Be careful," Fulton said as he looked at the building. "It looks like it has been closed for a long time."

"What is this place?" Ava asked as she walked to the unusually wide door.

"It's an old sawmill–they'd cut down the trees from the forest that surrounds us. Then they'd drag them here and use large saw blades inside this building to cut them into boards of wood so people could build things with them. Listen–you can hear the sound of running water. They used water to power the mill,"

Fulton said as they both pushed open the large door that let out a prolonged squeak from the rusty hinges.

They stepped inside the dimly lit building through the doorway that was covered in cob webs. Fulton waved his hand through the sticky strands that were layered in place anticipating errant insects. Daylight entered through several openings in the building. However, since the building was cluttered with antiquated industrial sawmill equipment, there were many shadows and dark areas throughout it. Fulton walked over to a wooden desk several feet from the door. He saw a faded calendar nailed to the wall which read: January 1933. Fulton studied the calendar for a few moments then pulled opened each drawer looking to see if he could find anything of interest. Ava walked over to the large conveyor system that would have carried the then newly-sawed boards of wood from the oversized circular saw blades that were located at the other end of the building. She marveled at the size of the building and looked across the machine frame of the long conveyor toward an opening that let daylight enter into one of the dark areas of the lifeless structure. Beyond the light, a shadowy figure could be seen behind a large wooden beam that was supporting the roof. It was a man wearing a dark gray suit and shiny black shoes. His face was hidden in the shadows. He was holding a dark brown barn swallow, and with a quick motion, snapped one of the wings of the docile bird before tossing it to the wooden floor. The injured bird landed within the illuminated area of the floor and flopped around struggling to get airborne. Ava spotted the bird moving about on the floor and immediately walked over to rescue it.

"Oh, NO. The poor thing is hurt," Ava said as she went under the conveyor machine and moved towards the bird.

"Be careful," Fulton said as he turned toward Ava.

The bird continued to flap one wing as it moved in a circular pattern. The injured bird moved toward the shadows by the wall as Ava approached it. She stepped on the spot where the bird had initially landed and took another step when there was a loud cracking sound and the floor collapsed under her. Ava screamed as she disappeared downward through the floor before Fulton's eyes. He rushed over to where she had been as her scream faded away to silence. Fulton stopped several feet away from where Ava last stood. He dropped to his knees and crawled the rest of the way using his hands to inspect the integrity of the floor as he advanced forward. Fulton reached the hole in the floor. He could see that the wooden floor had deteriorated from dry rot extending from the hole all the way to the wall. The opening on the wall not only let daylight in but also rain and snow. Over time, the wetness and drying effect weakened the strength of the wood. Fulton felt a cool breeze on his face coming up from the river below as he peered down through the hole in the floor. Fulton looked down at the river and along the riverbank for Ava. He yelled for her. He only heard the sound of the rushing water below. He sprang up from the floor and ran out the door. Fulton scrambled down an embankment then went under the sawmill building to the river to search for Ava.

Ava was already around the first bend of the river from the sawmill that passed through dense forest. She fought to keep afloat as the strong current seemed to push her side to side as it rushed downward. She gasped as she just missed slamming into a boulder that appeared from nowhere. The current picked up speed as she was dangerously tossed among large boulders that littered this narrow stretch of the river. She bobbed up and down as she moved along in the water. Ava was cold even though she continued to flail her arms about in a futile attempt to swim out of the grasp of the river. Her speed increased as the grade of the river followed the steep decline of the mountainside. She swallowed a mouthful of water as she was spun around back and forth as if she was in an industrial-sized washer machine. She coughed and struggled in the water as she moved even faster down the river. Her arms and legs were tired from struggling in the rough water and then her whole body became numb from the coldness of it. A moment later she felt weightlessness. She was floating in the air for a few seconds that abruptly changed to the terrifying feeling of falling. Water began to fall on her from above as she fell downward. She screamed as she fell more than forty feet to a swirling pool of water. The cascading waterfall pushed her under the water followed by the strong current which swept her down river. She was deposited unconscious onto a riverbank that was the far side of an elbow twist in the river. Her little body lay on the wet mud while her lower legs and feet were still in the water.

Meanwhile, Fulton was walking along the riverbank near the first bend of the river from the sawmill. He looked up and down the river. His heart raced from the fear that he may have lost Ava in the river with the worst possible outcome. He stopped at the water's edge, looked across the raging river, and up toward the trees.

"You pray now because a child has shamed you?" said an unknown voice that Fulton heard. He turned around expecting to see someone immediately behind him. There was no one there. He scanned the riverbank and the trees up the rocky slope as he walked a few steps away from the river. "Hello?!" Fulton said with a crack in his voice. There was no response. Fulton stared at the slope and the trees. He turned back to the river. Fulton gasped as an overwhelming burst of light occurred before him. His blood pressure soared while an incredible adrenaline rush passed through him. He was unable to fight or commit to flight. He was paralyzed not from fear but from awe.

Beyond the loud burbling sound of the rushing water, a whirring sound could be heard. A small green hummingbird appeared above Ava who was still unconscious on the riverbank. The wispy wings beat fifty times per second as it hovered above her face. It moved to her cheek brushing the tips of its wings against her skin. It then moved down to her ear and flicked the tip of its wing against Ava's ear lobe. The hummingbird let out a long chirping sound. Ava's eyes opened slowly. She raised her head up as the hummingbird flew backwards in front of her face.

"Hi," Ava said exhaustedly to the hummingbird while sitting up on her elbows.

The humming sound increased as the bird moved a few inches toward Ava then moved a few feet to the right of her.

"What are you doing little birdie?" Ava asked as she pulled her legs from the river and stood up onto the wet riverbank.

The hummingbird zoomed back and forth chirping loudly in front of her face as if it was trying to communicate to her. It zoomed forward a few feet than went back twice the distance. The hummingbird repeated this motion forward and twice the distance backward while it chirped loudly.

"What are you doing? Do you want me to follow you?" Ava asked.

The hummingbird zoomed forward at a fast speed and grabbed onto a small clump of Ava's hair then zoomed back until it stretched out tight. Ava's head jerked forward toward the forest.

"Owww! That wasn't very nice," Ava exclaimed as she stepped forward rubbing her head.

The hummingbird buzzed up above Ava then zoomed down behind her hitting her rear end with its long beak. "Ouch! You're very mean!" Ava yelled as she rubbed her rear end. The hummingbird chirped loudly and continued zooming toward Ava then backed away from her. "I'm coming. I coming. Gosh–you're so bossy," Ava said as she followed the hummingbird off the riverbank and up a rocky slope. At the top of the slope Ava stopped next to an evergreen fir tree. The hummingbird buzzed backwards past Ava, spun around, and hovered overlooking the river. "What'dya doing now?" Ava asked as she turned and looked down the slope. A large mottled-gray wolf appeared down near the river sniffing where Ava had been laying on the ground. Three more wolves, one black, one brown, and one gray-brown mix, arrived at the riverbank. Ava slowly stepped back from the slope as the hummingbird buzzed backwards. "Now I know what you were doing–you were saving me from them," Ava whispered to the hummingbird who fluttered rapidly up and down. Ava turned and ran through the forest with the hummingbird leading the way. The large gray wolf sniffed the ground following Ava's scent up the slope. It stopped as the slope became rocky. The alpha wolf moved along the slope looking for another way to reach the top of it to pursue Ava. The other wolves sniffing the ground followed the gray wolf.

The hummingbird led Ava through a grove of mature fir trees. She ran as fast as she could over the blanket of golden-brown fir needles that covered the ground. The years of defoliating needles piling up on the ground made it feel squishy soft as she ran over them. The thick cushion of fir needles silenced her steps but she quickly became tired from running uphill. Ava slowed down to a walk to catch her breath as the hummingbird began to buzz backwards then forward again attempting to move her faster. After a few more minutes of hiking, Ava and the hummingbird made it to the top of the hill that they were climbing. It was one of the several hills that surrounded the mountain that loomed above them. The hummingbird buzzed backwards and hovered in place. Ava looked back down the slope of the hill that they had just climbed.

Three quarters of the way down the hill, she saw a dark shadowy

figure that emerged from behind a tree then disappeared. Further

down the hill through the grove of fir trees, the wolves appeared

near the bottom of the slope. Their ears were upright, mouths open,

and were madly sniffing the ground for her scent. Ava and the

hummingbird moved backwards out of sight, turned, and ran down

the other side of the hill. She knew that the wolves were looking

for her. She had to find somewhere to hide from them. The

hummingbird flew ahead of Ava leading the way down the hill.

Her feet were moving so fast that she stumbled and fell to the

ground. She rolled over a few times then picked herself up and

continued running down the hill while avoiding the trees that

covered it.

The wolves were on top of the hill. Their noses were skimming the

ground then raised to the air. After a few deep snorts of air, the

gray wolf rushed to the edge of the hill and caught Ava's scent

from a breeze coming up the slope. He then pointed his eyes, ears, and nose to the target below before descending down the hill with the three other wolves fanning out behind him.

Ava reached the bottom of the hill. She ran across the open grassy area towards a tree that was growing in the middle of a group of large rocks. The hummingbird chirped loudly as they moved through the tall, white-yellow grass. They were halfway across the field when Ava thought that if she could climb the tree ahead of her, she'd be safe from the wolves. The wolves reached the bottom of the hill and quickly slipped into the tall grass without slowing down. They were fully committed to stalking their prey. Their ears were erect and forward while the mouths were still open but their tongues had retracted. Ava was tired from running, but saw that she was close to the rocks and the tree. She tripped on a low, uneven spot on the ground and fell down. She was exhausted and her legs were sore, but she pulled herself up again. She looked back and saw in the grass four upright tails of fur coming towards her. She ran as fast she could toward the rocks. Ava emerged from the grassy area and ran across a stretch of crushed gravel towards the rocks. Her heart was pounding in her chest as she got closer to the rocks. The hummingbird made a loud chirping noise as it moved upward a few feet, hovered in place, and then turned back toward the advancing wolves as if to say *Keep running Ava. I'll try to stop them.* Ava turned back to see where the wolves were and she stumbled on the uneven ground several yards from the rocks and tree. She had cuts on her face and was covered in dirt. She was too exhausted to run anymore. The wolves were spread out in a half-circle moving towards her and the rock formation. The hummingbird was hovering above Ava making a loud staccato chirping noise as if it was in danger. The large gray wolf emerged from the tall grass followed by the other three wolves. The gray wolf quickened its pace as it raced toward Ava who was kneeling on the ground with her eyes closed, and her head bowed to her folded hands. She whispered, "Lord Jesus Christ, Son of God, have mercy on me," as the gray wolf leapt at Ava's neck with its mouth open and canines bared while the black wolf attacked from the side. The gray wolf was stopped in mid-air inches from Ava's neck while the black wolf was stopped within two feet from her. Both wolves were suspended in the air and frozen in action. A moment later the black wolf was engulfed in flames that appeared to originate from within itself then turned to ash which was quickly dissipated into the air as it blew away. The gray wolf was cast backwards landing on the ground between the two remaining wolves. Ava, still kneeling, felt a comforting wave of warmth surround her. She opened her eyes and gasped. The gray wolf, two yards away from her, laid motionless and silent on the ground between the two other wolves. Both wolves, whimpering, were on the ground with their heads resting between their front paws.

"They will not harm you now," a voice said from behind Ava. She turned around, looked up and saw a man, with a closely trimmed beard, dressed in a blazing white linen robe with leather sandals, standing by himself.

"Did you do that?" Ava asked looking back to the wolves.

"You needed help," he responded.

"Thank you for saving me. Is he hurt?"

"Only sleeping. Go over and wake him. You'll be safe."

Ava got up and walked over to the wolves. She stopped as she stood over them and turned back to the man in the white robe.

"Do not be afraid," he said.

Ava reached down and touched the gray wolf's head. The wolf opened his eyes and let out a half-muted whimper. It crawled closer to Ava and licked her sock.

"Are you okay?" Ava asked as she patted his head and rubbed his back. The other two wolves lay silent. She reached out to comfort them.

"Ava–you cease to amaze me. They were determined to get you. Yet, you forgive them and have deep concern for their well-being."

Ava rubbed the backs of the two wolves that then turned to lick her hands. "They were just doing what they do. They didn't know it was wrong," she said. "They're probably just hungry. How do you know my name?"

"I know everything about you. I know your mother. I know your father."

Ava immediately thought about the many warnings she received at school from Sister Carmella and the other nuns about bad intentioned strangers stating that they "know" your parents in order to abduct children. She initially thought this could be one of those dangerous situations; however, she felt completely safe with this man.

"You are correct to be concerned about strangers. But truly I am not a stranger. I will bring you to Monsignor Fulton who is looking for you."

"What's your name?" Ava asked.

"There are many names that people use for me."

"What's your favorite?" Ava asked.

"During my time here, some of the ones that were close to me called me–Rabbouni."

"Oh, you're Italian like the boy in my school–Tommy Ravoni! I love spaghetti!" Ava said as she kept rubbing the backs of the wolves. "I'm sure you do, too."

"Come my child–we have a journey before us," Rabbouni said as he extended his hand to Ava who reached up and grabbed it. They walked through the tall grass with the wolves keeping pace beside them. A feint golden glow hung over them as they walked through the tall, white-yellow grass. Lush green grass appeared behind them which expanded outward like a rolling wave to the perimeter of the vast open field and followed them as they moved through the dry grass.

Chapter Six

It was mid-afternoon on the same day that Lewis had followed Fulton and Ava to the national park. After losing them on the mountain road in the forest, he decided to go back to Venice Beach. Lewis was standing on the steps outside of Desirea Jordan's apartment looking up at Roberta in the second-floor window.

"I'm a friend of Monsignor Fulton. He's expecting me. Well, I'm actually a little late. I missed the connecting flight–the airline lost my luggage," Lewis said as he was cut off from continuing his tale.

"Save your breath and <u>my time</u>! If it's all the same to you–I'd rather wait until your sad story becomes a book. You missed them.

They already left–early this morning," Roberta said as she tried to control her usual abrasive comments because of Lewis' supposed connection to Fulton. She didn't want to do anything that would jeopardize her prayer request that she had made to Fulton the day before.

"They're gone? You mean–they left for Vegas?" Lewis asked as he fished for information that would confirm his hunch.

"Yeah, they've gone to Vegas," Roberta said as she clenched her teeth and gripped the windowsill in an attempt to prevent herself from reaching the point when she typically would use harsh language laced with profanity instructing people to go away.

"Oh, boy! His phone number is on my cell phone that's in my luggage that's lost somewhere. I don't know where in Vegas I'm supposed to meet them."

"They shouldn't be too hard to find. There's only one bishop in Las Vegas," Roberta said as she rolled her eyes.

Lewis thanked Roberta for her time and drove away in his car. He reached for his smartphone and tapped several times on the screen before putting it to his ear.

"He's taken the kid to Vegas. It was just confirmed. Let's run with the story that he's taken a child out of state that has been put in the custody of the city, and he's defying a court order. Then we'll leak on social media that it's his kid. That'll do some damage, huh? I'm driving to Vegas now to catch up with them. I'll call you later," Lewis said then dropped his smartphone on the passenger front seat.

Ms. Pratt was holding a multi-page document as she strutted down the middle of the empty hallway in Fontbonne Academy. Her heavy footsteps echoed off the walls. She pushed open the door to the principal's office and entered the outer office area as if she was seizing control. Ms. Logan was standing by a file cabinet slipping several papers into a folder.

"Where's the principal?! I have a court order for her," Ms. Pratt barked as she stood at the counter. She knocked her knuckles against the top of the counter. "Hurry it up! This is official city business!"

Sister Carmella appeared in her doorway as Ms. Logan walked away from the filing cabinet.

"Calm down, Ms. Pratt. What is the purpose of your visit today?" Sister Carmella said.

Ms. Logan walked around the counter and over to Sister Carmella. She handed the three-page document to her.

"That's a court order for you to turn Ava Marie Rose over to ME! If you do not, you will be in violation of the court order and subject to arrest! So, will WE have your cooperation in this matter, or will I have to use law enforcement personnel?!" Ms. Pratt said as she folded her arms and leaned her weight to one leg.

Sister Carmella carefully read the document and upon completion looked up toward Ms. Pratt and said, "I have read the court order and understand the requirements."

"So, you will cooperate?" Ms. Pratt stated as she raised her eyebrows and nodded her head as if she was compelling the desired response from Sister Carmella.

"I'm unable to," Sister Carmella said.

"This is outrageous! This a direct violation of the court order! You've done it now! You'll be going to court!" Ms. Pratt exclaimed as her head shook side to side.

"Ms. Pratt, the court order has not been violated by me or the school. The fact of the matter is–Ava Marie Rose is not here," Sister Carmella said.

"Where is she?! You must tell me!" Ms. Pratt barked as her face turned crimson-red.

"The court order specifically states that Ava Marie Rose should be turned over if she is at our premises. She is not."

"You know where she is! You must tell me where she is!" Ms. Pratt screamed as she stomped her feet.

"Ms. Pratt, I have complied with this court order. The current class period is about to end. The children will be in the hallway to go to their next class. Seeing what happened yesterday when you were here and how upset the children were–it would be best for you to leave the premises now."

Ms. Pratt was panting. She looked side to side then shot an angry look at Sister Carmella and said through her clenched yellow teeth, "We're going to court! This isn't over yet!" Ms. Pratt turned on her heels and stormed out of the office.

"She means it. She's going over to the court right now to make trouble for you," Ms. Logan said as she stepped closer to Sister Carmella.

"Ms. Logan, we have educated scores of students from this school that have gone on to be extremely successful attorneys. God shall provide one of them to defend us," Sister Carmella said as she walked back into her office. "I'll be on the phone looking for one."

Later that afternoon, Sister Carmella was in a large conference room at the law office of Marley and Tucker. She was sitting at a long wooden meeting table across from Monica Moore. Monica was in her mid-forties, plain looking, and had dark-brown hair. She was wearing a gray business suit.

"The Division of Child Services has filed a motion for the court to issue a contempt of court finding on the school and has named you as the primary obstruction to the court order," Monica said as she looked up from writing on a yellow legal pad.

"What do you think about that?" Sister Carmella said as she sat forward at the edge of her chair with her hands folded on the table.

"Judge Silver, who issued the court order, has a history of supporting city and state authorities in these matters deeming them best suited to decide the common good for all parties involved," Monica said then revealed a facial expression of concern.

"I would still like you to file a motion that we take temporary custody of Ava at the school until her mother recovers enough to make a definitive parental decision," Sister Carmella said.

"I will file that motion. However, a more pressing issue is the contempt of court charge. This charge is something that the judge might react punitively if he feels that you blatantly disregarded the court order," Monica said as she slowly flipped her pen around her fingers.

"She left yesterday to visit her mother's aunt. The court order was issued today," Sister Carmella stated.

"Sister, I know that. My concern is if the judge asks you directly–did you send her to California to avoid the pending action of child services?"

"Oh–of course, I did."

"That's what I'm concerned about," Monica said as she raised her pen to highlight the point.

"It's the truth. I'm not ashamed of it–I will not lie."

"I know that Sister–and I wouldn't want you to," Monica said as she double tapped the pen on the pad of paper. "I need more background information. Please tell me about Ava's parents."

"Her mother was a student at the school. She graduated several years after you did," Sister Carmella said.

Ava's mother, Margie Lafolan, grew up in the Hell's Kitchen neighborhood on the west side of Midtown Manhattan, New York. Her mother, Diane, was a single parent and had one sister named Edna. Edna moved to California before graduating from high school and assumed a stage name–Desirea Jordan. Margie finished high school and then took a full-time position at a Midtown local insurance broker–Obrion and Russell. Obrion and Russell had a staff of fourteen people with most of them being in their forties and fifties. Margie was a cute blond with blue eyes who started out answering the telephone and soon was assembling quotes, binders, and policies for the brokers.

The brokers spent most of their time eating and drinking with clients. However, every Friday after work, the brokers took the clerical staff and broker assistants out for a drink to reaffirm their appreciation of the efforts made by the entire office. This appreciation consisted of draft beer and unlimited bowls of mixed nuts at the not-so-swanky Dugout Bar which was located in the basement of the same building they worked in.

In the insurance industry, the last day and the first day of the month are the busiest days of binding risk coverage. It was at an after-work gathering on the last Friday night in June, 2001 that Margie met Charlie Rose. The Obrion and Russell employees occupied the back section of the narrow bar. Margie walked the empty plastic pitcher to the bar to get a refill of beer. She stood by a young man in his mid-twenties with close-cropped blond hair. He was sipping a beer while watching a baseball game on the television that was attached to the wall. Margie stole a few glances of him while she looked down the bar to get the bartender's attention. She looked at his muscular arm then back up to his side profile. She looked forward and wondered if she should stay for another pitcher of beer as she focused on her reflection in the wall-sized mirror above the bar. She quickly realized that not only has the beer already impaired her mental faculties but, worse–the man standing beside her was looking at her and most likely saw her checking him out. Margie blushed.

"Did you want to fill that up?" the young man asked her as she held the empty beer pitcher.

"Umm, yeah. But, it's not for me. I mean–I'm not drinking it by myself," Margie said as the draft beer that had been sitting in her empty stomach was now making her head seem fuzzy.

"I know. You're with your family–over there," he said motioning with his head toward the back section of the bar.

"My family?! They're not my family," she said as she giggled.

"Oh, they're not–you sure?"

"Mm-huh. I'm very sure. They're not," she said then laughed.

"Oh, because I do see a family resemblance you have with a few of them," he said as he took another sip of beer.

"What?! Which one?! They're OLD!" Margie yelled as she covered her mouth and looked over to her co-workers motioning that she's getting the beer. She turned back to the bar as she felt a funny tingling feeling in her belly that went to her head that was not from the alcohol.

"What's your name?"

"Margie."

"I'm Charlie Rose," he said as he extended his hand to her. "It's a pleasure to meet you, Margie."

She shook his hand and said, "Nice to meet you, Charlie Rose. Are you here with friends?"

"No, by myself. I'm on my first day of vacation."

"On vacation–by yourself?!"

"Yeah. I like to travel alone. That way I can see the things I want to and take my time."

"What do you do for work?"

"I'm in the Army,"

"Really–the Army?! How many days of vacation did you get?"

"Fifty-nine hours left on a three-day pass." Charlie said as he glanced down at his watch.

"Your Army base must be close to here then?" she said as she studied his eyes and face.

"I'm down at Fort Bragg in North Carolina. Never been to New York City. Always wanted to see it. So, I'm here."

"Did you get to see anything today?"

"You. That's it for me. That's all that I needed to see. As soon as I finish my beer–I'm just going back to Fort Bragg. Best vacation–ever," Charlie said as he took another sip of his beer.

Margie smiled and said, "Have you seen anything else; Statue of Liberty, Empire State Building?"

Charlie shook his head and said, "Nope."

"You haven't seen Central Park?!"

"Is that a parking garage?" Charlie asked, jokingly.

"No!" Margie exclaimed followed by a loud laugh as she then sheepishly looked over toward her co-workers.

"It doesn't matter anyways–I flew. Took a taxi here from the airport."

She giggled and said, "You're only kidding with me now. You know what Central Park is, right?"

"I know what it is. But I've never seen it. And I would like to see it with you," Charlie said as he looked into her eyes. "Will you please go out to dinner with me tonight, and after we can go see Central Park?"

Margie stared into his green eyes and swallowed hard. "Yes," she said softly as she bit her bottom lip. Charlie took the empty pitcher from her and placed it on the bar. He tossed a twenty-dollar bill on the bar. He motioned for the bartender to fill up the pitcher with beer for her co-workers as she waved good-bye to them.

Margie and Charlie went out to dinner and walked along a beautiful green leafy tree lined road through Central Park holding hands as the warm summer sun began to set behind the skyline of city buildings. They took a horse-drawn open carriage ride through the park. Over the next two days, Margie and Charlie squeezed in so many classic New York tourist destinations that she didn't spend much time at home. Her mother was concerned that her daughter was moving too quickly with a man she just met. Margie drove Charlie to the airport Sunday evening so she could spend more time with him. They had already made plans for her to fly down to Fort Bragg the following weekend.

"The only reason that I'm getting on that plane is because if I don't–the MPs will come looking for me and stick me in Leavenworth. Then I'd never get to see you," Charlie said as he hugged her tight and kissed her on her forehead.

"Oh, I wish you didn't have to go. I know I'll see you in five days, but I just don't want to wait that long," Margie said as she looked up to Charlie and kissed him on his lips. "Can't you quit?"

"I signed up for four years. It would've been different had I met you before."

Margie and Charlie continued their long embrace as an announcement was made over the airport PA system for the final boarding call to Fayetteville, North Carolina. Charlie picked up his bag and walked down the jetway looking back to wave one more time to Margie. She waved back to him and moved over to the large windows to watch the jet pushback then roll onto to the runway. Their whirlwind romance had begun and she was determined to ride it out no matter where it ended.

Charlie grew up in Westerly, Rhode Island and was adopted as an infant by an older couple named Betty and Bob Rose. Bob Rose was retired from managing the grounds and facilities at the state hospital school located in Westerly. Betty retired as the clerical manager at an electronics manufacturing company. Charlie was their only child and they adored him. Charlie took a job in construction after graduating from the local high school. Although it was hard work, it was good money for a young man.

In 2000, early February, Bob Rose had a sudden heart attack that took his life. Betty was devastated. She had lost her childhood sweetheart and the man she had been married to for forty-six years. The void and the heartbreak she felt from losing her husband was too great for her. She passed away nine months later; a week before Thanksgiving. Betty and Bob were the only family Charlie had and now they were gone. He was twenty-four years old and completely devastated with the loss of his parents. He mulled around Westerly and continued working construction for the next several weeks.

In early January, he decided that he needed a change and it would be significant. He was going to sell the only house he ever lived in and join the Army. One month later he was fully engaged in the infantry training program at Fort Bragg in North Carolina. Charlie welcomed the order that the military provided and the distraction from his heartache from losing his parents. This comfort in order was now upended with meeting Margie; he couldn't stop thinking about her and dreaded being so far away from her.

Margie was always close to her mother, Diane. She was a single parent since the moment she gave birth to Margie. Diane never spoke about the man who fathered Margie, not even to her sister Edna. Margie accepted early in life that her mother would never tell her about her father. The most she ever said to Margie is the night she came back from driving Charlie to the airport. Margie told her mother how she felt about Charlie and leaving him at the airport made her sick to her stomach. Her mother said for her to be prepared for possible disappointment with Charlie because young men in the military tend to move around a lot and fall in love as much. Margie had a strong feeling that her mother's comment was a hidden personal reflection about her own father. Margie asked her mother if her father was in the military. Her response was only that she hoped that Charlie wouldn't break her heart.

Over Labor Day weekend, Charlie received a three-day pass for a high score in a special operations and tactics training program. He flew up to New York on Friday evening and met Margie's mother who initially was coldly reserved. By Sunday afternoon when it was time for him to go to the airport for his return flight, she had warmed to a smile and welcomed him back anytime. A week from that Tuesday, the world changed for everyone when passenger planes were hijacked and used as weapons of mass destruction. Charlie was activated into a Special Forces Unit that would be sent off to combat in Afghanistan less than a month later.

By the spring of 2002, Charlie had returned to Fort Bragg in North Carolina and was back in New York as soon as he was issued a few days leave. Soon, Charlie and Margie were married and moved into a standard military housing complex at Fort Bragg. In 2003, early March, Charlie's unit was activated for the Iraq invasion. He was camped in Kuwait until the invasion began a few weeks later. He came home for Christmas that year and delayed another deployment to Iraq the following spring by signing up for another four years in the army. He would be assigned to a training role at Fort Bragg. Charlie never discussed his combat experience to Margie other than saying he didn't see much action. She didn't believe him and thought that he said that so she wouldn't be worried. Margie and Charlie enjoyed life together over the next year at the base in North Carolina.

In April 2005, they welcomed the birth of their baby girl named Ava Marie. Charlie loved his daughter so much it seemed that he never put her down. Two months later, Charlie was redeployed to Iraq where his unit experienced fierce combat against a strong insurgency.

In early 2006, he returned back home hoping that he wouldn't be sent back to Iraq. Charlie was all done with the military life. He just wanted to spend time with Margie and their baby girl, Ava. They moved to a single-family house on the base that had a small backyard with a large patch of grass that was equally mixed with weeds, an oversized oak tree with an old tire hanging from a long rope, and a weathered wooden picket fence outlining the property. Charlie hung several hummingbird feeders up in the backyard and one against the wall of their screened porch. He and Ava spent hours watching the different hummingbirds zoom in and out to feed on their homemade sugar and water solution.

"Daddy, why do they fly funny?" Ava asked as she pressed her face against the screen.

"God made them special," Charlie said as he held her in his arms and watched a purple hummingbird fly backwards away from the feeder.

"Are they from heaven?"

"I think they are," Charlie said as he kissed her forehead.

"Are they good, Daddy?"

"Yes, they are. When I'm at work–they watch over you for me," Charlie said as Ava quickly turned her head away from watching the hummingbirds and looked at him with her eyes wide opened.

"They do?! They watch over me?" Ava asked with great surprise that ended in a whisper.

Charlie chuckled and said, "Yeah–I asked them to keep an eye on you and keep you out of trouble." He brushed her hair from her face and kissed her cheek.

Ava turned back to the hummingbirds and said, "They're my guardian angels."

Charlie was ordered back to Iraq to train elite Iraqi soldiers for counterinsurgency operations. Margie was worried more with this particular assignment than she ever was in any of his other combat assignments. She didn't know why she felt this way. It was just something deep down in her stomach that made her feel that something was different. Charlie assured her that he would not be in any combat operations in Iraq. He explained that he would be segregated within a high security base and only interact with handpicked soldiers for special training. Charlie went on to say that these nine months will be like having a baby, and this time, it'll be a very happy Charlie Rose coming home for good. He told Margie that they could move to New York if she wanted to be near her mother. He didn't care; he just wanted to get back to having a normal life with the two people he loved most in the world. Charlie made Ava promise that she would keep feeding the hummingbirds while he was away. Ava raised her hand as if she was taking an oath and swore that she would feed them.

A month later, Ava was still feeding the hummingbirds. In fact, she insisted on mixing the sugar and water herself while standing on a chair by the sink as Margie stood next to her.

"We have to hurry up, Ava. Nanna's coming to stay with us." Margie said.

"Nanna can help me feed the hummingbirds," Ava said as she spilled some of the sugar and water mix in the sink.

The doorbell rang and Margie helped Ava step down from the chair.

"Nanna's here!" Ava exclaimed.

Margie walked to the door while Ava carefully held the pitcher of sugar and water mix in her hands as she followed her mother to the door. Margie gasped as she stepped back covering her mouth and started to cry. Two brawny men wearing US Army green service uniforms with solemn faces were standing at the front door.

"What's the matter, Mommy?!" Ava asked as she looked at her mother with great concern. "Why are you crying, Mommy?!" She then turned to the two men who were still standing at the front door and asked, "Where's my Daddy?"

The two soldiers, dreading the most difficult assignment for anyone in the military which became unfathomably worse with the presence of Ava, swallowed hard as they silently stepped into the house and slowly closed the front door.

Chapter Seven

The Ynez-Aztecan Reservation was located in a large, flat arid valley in southeastern California near the Nevada border. The Ynez River flows through the reservation and was the reason the Ynez-Aztecan Indian Tribe settled there several hundred years ago. The peak size of the tribe was 14,000 people. The tribe's population had been hollowed out over the centuries from disease, war, starvation, no productive economy, alcoholism, and drug use. There were only a few hundred tribal members living on the reservation and a small group of elders still practicing the traditions of their ancestors.

Wednesday afternoon, Sachem Whitehorse was standing by a large fire surrounded by rocks. Three tribal elders were sitting around the fire chanting while Whitehorse raised his hand to the air. Two younger men came out of an old cinder block house that was located among several other buildings. They were in their mid-twenties and each was holding a can of beer.

"What are they doing?" Tommy asked as they walked over to his beat-up pickup truck.

"Being crazy. They've been sitting there since yesterday staring at the fire," Dakota said. He was the grandson of Sachem Whitehorse.

"I thought they were burning trash," Tommy said.

"Yesterday, I woke up and the old man said that he had a vision about the Great Spirit. He was talking crazy—we must prepare the land. We must clean our bodies and minds. He started rapping that Ynez crap. I just walked away," Dakota said then dismissively waved his hand downward at them.

The two young men were sitting on the open tailgate of Tommy's pickup truck.

"What time are we gonna meet them?" Dakota asked.

"We gotta be at the border before one. Should take about four hours to get there," Tommy said.

"We moving personas or maiz?" Dakota asked.

Tommy laughed. "Yeah, white corn! You know, I bet you someone whacked-out has had a corn or two! Come on, let's get something to eat."

Tommy and Dakota were laughing as they got into the pickup truck and drove away. Meanwhile, the elders that were sitting around the fire, suddenly stood up near Whitehorse. They watched as three wolves approached them from the ravine below followed by Rabbouni and Ava.

A young Ynez-Aztecan girl named Peque was introduced to Ava by her grandfather who was one of the elders. Peque was seven years old. She was cute with short black hair. Peque, Ava, and the wolves went down to the Ynez River to play while Rabbouni stayed with the elders. Walking along the riverbank, Ava found a dead bird that was already stiff from rigor mortis. She picked up the bird and ran back to Rabbouni.

Ava, with tears running down her face, stood nearby while Rabbouni spoke to the elders. He stopped speaking and turned to Ava.

"Child, why do you cry?" Rabbouni asked.

"He's dead," Ava sniffled as she held the dead bird in her open hands.

"No, he's sleeping," Rabbouni responded.

The elders knew the bird was dead and were puzzled by Rabbouni's comment.

"Wake him. Fill your lungs with air," Rabbouni said as Ava took a deep breath of air. "Now, blow it out onto him."

The elders watched as Ava blew her breath on the bird. The delicate colorful feathers were ruffled from the quick blast of air. The bird twitched then opened its eyes. It slowly stood up in her open hands.

"Yeah!" Ava exclaimed as the bird let out a loud chirp then flew away. The elders were in awe and bowed their heads to Rabbouni.

A few hours after sunset that same day, thirty members of the tribe were sitting by the fire. They were of varying ages and occupied approximately 240 degrees around the fire. They left the remaining space for Rabbouni who sat by himself on a large rock. Rabbouni spoke to them about their ancestors. The people assembled were spellbound by the details about their respective families spanning generations that he revealed to them.

Toward the back of the group, Peque's mother was sitting. She became more vocal and anxious as she looked around for her daughter. Another young girl said that she hadn't seen her for at least a half-hour. Peque's mother was in a complete panic. The disturbance began to spread and become louder as people sitting closer to the fire looked back at her. Rabbouni looked across the fire and over the heads of the people sitting in a semicircle around it. He made eye contact with Peque's mother.

"My Peque is missing!" Peque's mother cried to Rabbouni.

Rabbouni looked over to his right where the three wolves were lying on the ground surrounding Ava. The two older wolves simultaneously sprung up when he made eye contact with them. A moment later, they ran off into the darkness behind where Rabbouni was sitting. The crowd was murmuring about the wolves and how they are controlled by Rabbouni without him speaking commands to them. Peque's mother cried.

"Do not be afraid; your child is safe," Rabbouni said to her.

"Where is she?!" Peque's mother pleaded.

"In the desert, behind me," Rabbouni said as he looked at her.

Several feet away from Rabbouni, a rectangular shape of light appeared in the darkness. It was five feet wide by six feet tall from the ground. The crowd gasped when it appeared. The rectangular shape of light then rapidly extended outward making a corridor of light in a straight line into the desert. The running wolves appeared in the corridor of expanding light as it went farther into the desert. The crowd continued to gasp and wonder at this amazing scene before them. The expanding corridor of light ended approximately 1,500 yards away from the camp fire.

"Peque!" Peque's mother cried out as two other women consoled her.

"The wolves have found her and are bringing her back to you," Rabbouni said.

The corridor of light began to collapse back toward the crowd.

"The light–it's shrinking!" a woman exclaimed.

The corridor of light was collapsing back faster than it had originally expanded. The entrance of the rectangular-shaped corridor of light near Rabbouni grew brighter as it collapsed back toward the crowd. They began to squint and shield their eyes from the intense brightness. The brightness dimmed at the entrance of the corridor of light then Peque appeared followed by the two wolves. The crowd gasped as Peque's mother ran over to her and hugged her.

"I got lost, Mommy! I was so scared! Then the wolves found me and carried me back," Peque exclaimed to her mother.

Later that evening, in a small bedroom at Sachem Whitehorse's house, Rabbouni stood over the small bed that Ava was lying in.

"Why can't you stay here? I'll sleep on the floor," Ava said to him.

"I must talk to more people. You will be safe here," Rabbouni said.

"Please–let me go with you, Rabbouni," Ava pleaded.

"You must stay here for now. But I will give you something for comfort and to dream about," Rabbouni said as a black cat leaped onto her bed. It had a white marking on its chest and a clipped left ear.

"Mumma Cat!" Ava exclaimed as she rolled over to her side to get closer to the cat.

"She will keep you company until I return," Rabbouni said as the cat walked over to Ava's face and bumped her head against Ava's head.

"Oh, Mumma Cat–it is you!" Ava said as she hugged the cat. "Where have you been?! You've been gone for so long. How did you get here? Did you go on an airplane, too?"

Two years ago, Ava's cat had strayed from the house one night and fell victim to a roaming coyote searching for food.

Meanwhile, in Las Vegas, Fulton was walking down the Las Vegas Strip with its dazzling neon lights and colorful people. Singles, couples, and families walked along the famous boulevard sharing the sidewalk with drug users, con artists, and prostitutes. Scantily dressed women walked through the crowd which included young children. Loud music and the smell of burning marijuana filled the desert air as hustlers handed out business cards with pictures of nude women. Celebrity look-alikes and people dressed in costumes walked around for pictures for a pressured fee.

Fulton had never been to Las Vegas and was appalled by what he was seeing. It reminded him of the ancient cultures throughout human history just before their inevitable destruction. He walked along until he came upon a crowd that was waiting for the high-tech volcano to erupt outside one of the larger casinos. He stood among the people and listened to them talk about being drunk, high on drugs, and various pleasures of the flesh they had experienced in the city.

"Would you destroy it all?" a voice said to Fulton.

Fulton looked to his right to see who was talking to him. The person next to him was hugging a young lady as they watched the volcano show. Fulton looked behind and to his left to see if anyone was speaking to him. The crowd cheered at the music and special effects as everyone watched the spectacle of the erupting volcano.

"Would you destroy the world and every living thing, James?" a voice said to Fulton. He turned to his right and saw Rabbouni standing beside him. Fulton gasped then felled to his knees.

"Lord, every life is precious," Fulton stammered out his reply as the crowd of people carried on celebrating the fantastic show. It appeared that the crowd did not see or hear Fulton or Rabbouni.

"But you were just thinking how this city and the world is like Sodom and Gomorrah. That you would expect the Father Almighty to extinguish it," Rabbouni said.

"Lord, I came here as you instructed me when I saw you at the river. I've lost an innocent little girl who may have drowned. I'm still trying to understand your presence. I'm concerned that I'm hallucinating and that I've gone insane," Fulton said with tears streaming down his face as he looked up to Rabbouni.

"James, you are not insane. I told you before that Ava was with me. Your frustration with church hierarchy regarding the abuse of children and the never-ending failure of humans to be kind to one another has you questioning everything you know and believe," Rabbouni said.

Their conversation occurred in the presence of the crowd; however, the crowd could not see them nor hear them. Fulton could see the crowd around him and their chatter could be heard as if he was on the other side of a glass wall.

"From scripture, when you return–it means the end of days. Lord, is that now?" Fulton asked.

"Only the Father Almighty knows and then I know. You shall go with me tonight," Rabbouni said. "There are more to gather."

The crowd cheered and screamed as the erupting volcano show ended. The invisible membrane surrounding Rabbouni and Fulton was gone. The people around Fulton looked down at him. He was still kneeling on the ground.

"You okay, mister?" said the young man who had been hugging his girlfriend.

Fulton stood up and mumbled something to them while Rabbouni walked away along the sidewalk. Fulton hurried after him. Rabbouni walked down the middle of the crowded sidewalk then crossed the vehicle congested multi-lane boulevard. The traffic stopped and no car horns could be heard. Fulton followed him across the busy street and stopped at the sidewalk. Rabbouni walked up to a small group of people that were off to the side and somewhat in the shadows. There was a large man that was covered in tattoos standing by another man that had a slight build and was several inches shorter. He was yelling at two young women that were wearing revealing clothing and high heels.

"You gotta bad frigg'in attitude! You gonna get something for that!" the lean man yelled as he stepped toward the two young ladies. He raised his fist to his shoulder as the woman who had long black hair, named Kimba, stepped forward shielding the other woman who had short blond hair.

"We were working!" Kimba yelled.

"Why don't you try it for a while?!" Jackie yelled as she pulled Kimba back from the lean man.

"Listen to that! Bad attitudes and big mouths!" the lean man said as he stepped forward and swung his fist at Kimba as she closed her eyes for the impact. Jackie screamed as she pulled Kimba back causing them to fall to the ground. They huddled together to protect themselves from the expected beating. A few moments later, they saw black ash falling around them. They looked up and saw Rabbouni standing above them.

"You know what you do is wrong. Do you want to change your life forever?" Rabbouni asked them.

Kimba and Jackie nodded their heads as tears ran down their faces.

"Come with me and you will have a life of happiness that will last forever," Rabbouni said.

Fulton, Kimba, and Jackie followed Rabbouni down the street. A homeless man was passed out drunk on the sidewalk. As Rabbouni walked by the homeless man, he woke up, stood up, then joined the small group that walked behind Rabbouni. They walked toward the entrance of a grand casino. Rabbouni entered the opulent lobby followed by his diverse entourage. They walked past security personnel and dozens of casino visitors that barely noticed them.

Rabbouni entered the brightly lit casino where the rows of slot machines were located. As he walked down the main aisle the sound of slot machine bells rang out and neon lights flashed followed by the recorded noise of coins falling into a thin metal coin tray. Dozens of people were waving winning paper tickets from the slot machines and yelled with glee. This phenomenon moved like a large wave throughout the casino as Rabbouni continued to pass through it. He then walked by the Blackjack tables and Crap tables. Everyone gambling was winning. The casino pit bosses and managers reached for their two-way radios and hand microphones to communicate with people in the high-tech security room to understand what was going on. The cheering and yelling permeated the entire casino and continued outside as Rabbouni exited. People rushed into the casino to place a bet.

"What's happening?" Jackie asked Kimba as Fulton looked around the casino watching everyone winning slot machine tickets and casino chips.

Fulton hurried through the casino to catch up to Rabbouni who was walking down the Las Vegas Strip. Each casino Rabbouni passed along the sidewalk was transformed into a wild betting frenzy with every gambler winning at the expense of the casino. Each casino would respond to this strange mass winning phenomena by closing down all its gambling operations.

The next morning in the Manhattan Family Courthouse, Sister Carmella and Monica Moore were sitting at the defense table in the courtroom. Ms. Pratt and two prosecuting attorneys from the City Attorney's Office sat at the prosecutor's table. Ms. Pratt was staring forward toward the judge who was reading the prosecutor's charges in the case. The older prosecutor, who had a bushy mustache with waxed tips that were twisted outward to a point, was explaining some elements of the case to the younger female prosecutor with shoulder-length brown hair and a dark-blue business suit.

"This seems straight forward to me. When the child returns from visiting her relative in Los Angeles, she should be turned over to the city's child services department for care and custody," Judge Silver said as he looked up from the documents.

Monica Moore stood up and raised her hand. "Your honor, on behalf of my client, we request that this court wait until we hear from the child's nearest relative–Desirea Jordan, who has a recorded interest in the care and custody of the child if the mother remains incapacitated," she said.

"What is this recorded interest?" Judge Silver asked looking over his eyeglasses that were resting on the tip of his long-pointed nose.

"The student emergency and medical document that each student has on file at the school. It details primary and secondary persons allowed to care for the child in case of an emergency or medical issue. The mother of the child in question has designated Desirea Jordan as the person who can assume responsibility of Ava Marie

Rose in case of an emergency or medical issue," Monica Moore said as she held a document in her hand.

"May I see a copy of that?" Judge Silver requested.

"Yes, your honor," Monica Moore said as she stepped forward and provided a copy to Judge Silver. On her way back to her seat she walked over to the prosecutor's table and provided a copy of the same document to the older prosecutor. Ms. Pratt's stone-face had turned angry when the document was presented to the judge.

The judge carefully read the document as the bow-tied prosecutor quickly scanned his copy. Ms. Pratt leaned over the younger prosecutor, and with great exasperation, whispered to the older prosecutor. He nodded his head and stood up. "Your honor, this is not a last will of testimony. Moreover, we do not know the mental capacity and capability of this Desirea Jordan. Furthermore, Ms. Jordan lives in Los Angeles and uprooting the child and moving her 3,000 miles away from her routine would be detrimental to her

well-being to say the least," the older prosecutor said as Monica
Moore stood up from her chair.

"Your honor, it's my understanding that Ms. Jordan is of sound
mind, capable, and interested in the care and custody of the child.
It is also my understanding, that she would not relocate the child
and would make the necessary arrangements for Ava Marie Rose
to continue to reside in New York," she said.

"The permanent custody can be decided at some point in the
future. There is a more immediate need to identify the interim
steward for care and custody," Judge Silver said.

"Your honor, as you know, the child is with her next of kin that
has been designated by her mother and will be returning after their
trip is completed," Monica Moore said.

"She's not with her relative! She is driving around California
with a stranger!" Ms. Pratt exclaimed as the older prosecutor was
startled from her outburst.

The judge looked over to Monica Moore for a response.

"Your honor, the child was escorted from the school to her relative by Monsignor James Fulton who oversees all of the schools in the Archdiocese system in the State of New York. We know from Monsignor Fulton that Ava Marie Rose was brought to Ms. Jordan's home two days ago," Monica Moore said.

"That's a lie! He's taking her to Las Vegas!" Ms. Pratt exclaimed as the older prosecutor motioned with his hand for her to quiet down. The judge looked over to the defense for a response.

"We do not have the child's daily schedule while she's visiting with her aunt. And it's not unusual for people to travel while visiting family and friends. In fact, I would expect that she may visit Disneyland and other destinations while she's away," Monica Moore said.

"When is the child expected back from her visit?" Judge Silver asked.

Monica Moore leaned over to Sister Carmella; they whispered to each other.

"She is expected to return next week," Monica Moore said.

"Do you have a date? Will the aunt be coming with the child to New York?" Judge Silver asked.

"Your honor, we will find out and get back to you on that," Monica Moore said.

"What about the gross violation of the court order?! They sent the adolescent away–defying the court order!" Ms. Pratt exclaimed as the older prosecutor winced from her outburst.

"Your honor, Ava Marie Rose left for California the day before the court issued the order. We request that the charge of noncompliance to the court order be dismissed," Monica Moore stated.

"It's a lie! They knew it was coming!" Ms. Pratt exclaimed as spit flew from her mouth as the older prosecutor pursed his lips and shifted his weight in his seat.

"Your honor, at this time I would like to submit to the court, a police report that details the aggressive and violent actions made by Ms. Pratt and a member of her agency against a faculty member and several elementary students at Fontbonne Academy before the court order was issued," Monica Moore said as she stood up with copies of the document. She walked to the judge's bench and handed a report to him then provided a copy to the surprised older prosecutor.

"We have standing authority to take custody of adolescents that are unsupervised! They attacked us!" Ms. Pratt shuddered as she explained her position.

The older prosecutor and the judge read the police report.

"I would like to spend more time reviewing this police report and give the city agency some time to respond to it. Let's continue this tomorrow morning–Friday at ten o'clock. Then we can address the issue of noncompliance to the court order. Both sides should be prepared to provide testimony," Judge Silver said as he made eye contact with Monica Moore.

Chapter Eight

Early Thursday morning in Las Vegas, Duval Lewis was standing on the sidewalk talking on his smartphone phone.

"I'm outside the casino, right now. I paid the security manager five hundred bucks to see the video surveillance from last night. I saw Fulton walking into the casino with two prostitutes and some homeless wino–then everything goes crazy. Everyone gambling in the place–WINS! You know, that goes against their business model! Casinos are not supposed to lose anything beyond some chump change. Fulton and his crew walked in–then walked out– then went down the street. Every casino on the strip closed down– they were all losing money. Everyone gambling was winning! It was the craziest thing! The security manager said he still hasn't been told yet if the casino will open today. They think it was some type of coordinated cyberattack. I'm still looking for Fulton–I'll call you back when I find him," Duval Lewis said as he walked down the street toward the next casino. There was no video footage of Rabbouni with Fulton and the others when they were in the casino or walking along the strip.

Meanwhile, on the Ynez-Aztecan Reservation, Fulton stepped out from an old cinder block house. He held a hand above his eyes and squinted from the bright light of the morning sun. Fulton wondered where he was and how he got here from Las Vegas. He smelt the smooth, dried wood that was burning as he walked toward a group of elderly men sitting around a fire that was surrounded by large stones.

"He has gone to the river," Whitehorse said to Fulton.

Fulton almost asked him who he was talking about but instinctively knew who it had to be.

"He said that some people will be coming to see you," Whitehorse said.

"When are they coming?" Fulton asked.

"They're here now," Whitehorse said as he raised his hand toward another adobe structure that was further away.

Teddy Webster, Jim, Pedro, and Juan walked toward Fulton as they looked around assessing the situation and trying to recognize someone.

"Is he here?" Teddy Webster asked as he looked at everyone near the fire.

"Who are you looking for?" Fulton said.

"Are you Fulton?" Juan asked.

"Yes. How did you know my name?" Fulton asked.

"He told me–ah, us–that we would find you here," Juan said.

"How did you get here?" Fulton asked.

The four men looked at each other and were trying to make sense of how they arrived there.

"That's the thing–we don't know how we got here. We woke up out there," Juan said as he motioned with a slight nod of his head toward the desert, "and saw these houses in the distance and figured that you'd be here."

"He told us your name and that we would find you here. Well, we think he told us. We all had the same dream–he told us that you would be here," Teddy Webster said.

"Where the heck are we?" Jim asked Fulton. "I'm so hungry."

Fulton looked over to Whitehorse for the answer as Jackie and Kimba emerged from another weathered white-washed adobe structure twenty feet away from the one he had woke up in.

The Ynez River had been reduced in width and its flow of water over the past several decades from the growing water consumption by communities located far from the reservation. Historically, the river was approximately one hundred feet across with a depth of three feet to four feet throughout the year. The river was now less than half of its original width and depth. The sloping banks framed the dry riverbed areas along the narrowed river. Rocks and some large boulders were strewn along the exposed riverbed.

It was midmorning and a perfect temperature of 72 degrees Fahrenheit. Low-hanging wispy fog floated along the river. By the river, a large group of people were sitting on a relatively flat open area that was shaded by a grove of black oak trees. Rabbouni was standing before them about several feet up on the gradual slope of the riverbank. On each side of him, about ten feet away, were two large black oak trees that had taken root into a collapsed section of the riverbank. The tree trunks were three feet in diameter and looked like columns from an ancient temple.

There were seventy people listening to Rabbouni. They were a diverse group in age, ethnicity, and social position. They sat on the ground spellbound as Rabbouni spoke to them. He was charismatic and exuded an aura of holiness that made everyone completely calm.

Rabbouni turned to one particular person in the crowd. It was the highly-acclaimed scientist, Thomas Burchill who was a balding middle-aged man with a mustache and beard.

"You are a highly educated man of science–yet, you believe life and everything created in the universe was by random chance," Rabbouni said as he stared at Burchill. "You and your kind ridicule anyone that believes in miracles and that the universe was of divine creation. How do you reconcile through science that the slightest minute change in any of the four fundamental forces and the universe would have never been?! The creation of the universe is a miracle!"

Burchill didn't respond. He sat there thinking that he must be dreaming this encounter and being among these strangers.

"The irony of it–you sometimes question some of the dogma of your false religion but, you are too frightened to speak up–for the risk of exile is too great!" Rabbouni said to him then he spoke to the crowd. "People most often think about the importance of their lives while they devalue the lives of others. All life is precious and fragile. When life ends here–it does not mean life ends," Rabbouni said as he dabbed his fingertip on his tongue then outstretched his hand. He deposited less than a drop of his saliva into the air where it was suspended in place. The crowd watched as the microscopic spec of matter increased in size to a dark-reddish blob of matter that hung in the air surrounded by a transparent pinkish-red membrane sac.

The crowd gasped as the now basketball-sized matter expanded in the flexible transparent sac as it transformed into a strange grotesque-looking entity. The transparent sac expanded to three feet across as the strange looking entity continued to increase in size and shape. The transparent sac stretched down to the ground and then burst opened revealing a 200-pound baby woolly mammoth. The crowd let out a collective gasp. The newborn mammoth struggled to stand up as it increased in size before their eyes. It grew to twelve feet high at its shoulders and weighed six tons within several seconds. It had a huge domed head, large humped shoulders, and a sloping back. Finger sized ivory tusks quickly grew into thick curved ones that measured fourteen feet long. The woolly mammoth raised its long powerful trunk and let out a loud trumpet blast that startled the crowd with fear and wonder. It slowly walked away from Rabbouni and moved along the river stopping to graze on some grass.

"They've been extinct for ten thousand years!" a man exclaimed, who was from the crowd of seventy people. Some of the people in the crowd stood up to watch the woolly mammoth eat the grass.

Away from the crowd of seventy people, Ava was sitting next to Fulton and Teddy. She looked over to Fulton and said with a big smile, "That's a woolly mammoth, you know."

Fulton nodded his head and said, "It sure is." Fulton watched Rabbouni as he turned away from the crowd and walked toward them.

Juan, Pedro, and Jim were standing several feet away from Fulton while Jackie and Kimba were nearby. Rabbouni raised his hands outward as the seven of them stood before him. Ava was nearby playing with the wolves.

Later that day in Manhattan, Ms. Logan entered Sister Carmella's office holding a few pages that she had printed from a news website. Sister Carmella had just finished speaking on the telephone as Ms. Logan handed it to her. She slowly put the telephone handset down as she read the printed article.

"It's all lies! How can they print such things?!" Ms. Logan exclaimed as she stood by Sister Carmella's desk.

The online news article read: National Network reports Church Bigwig on the Run with Love Child. Vicar General of the NY Archdiocese takes his daughter out of church-run school for a vacation on the west coast then goes to gamble with prostitutes in Las Vegas casino.

Sister Carmella dropped the article on her desk and softly said, "Dear Lord."

"They're evil to print those lies! That poor little girl–hasn't she suffered enough?!" Ms. Logan said.

"That was our attorney–apparently the judge saw the same article and has issued an emergency care and custody order for Ava. He has requested that California and Nevada enforce the court order because of the immediate child endangerment issues. Child services will likely be granted custody of her now," Sister Carmella said as she stared at the article on her desk.

"Oh, that's a shame! That sweet girl. She's already had so many hardships. Is Monsignor Fulton in trouble?" Ms. Logan said.

"Not for taking Ava out to see her relative. But, it's these malicious untruths and how the church responds that concerns me. Well, we must pray on it. It's not over yet–we still have to be in court tomorrow," Sister Carmella said as she pushed the article to the left corner of her desk.

Burchill walked away from the crowd of seventy people and over to Fulton and the others.

"Where did he go?" Burchill asked as he pulled out a smartphone from his pocket.

"For a walk. He said he'd be back soon," Fulton said.

"It won't work out here," Juan said motioning to Burchill's smartphone. "There's no reception."

"I know–I already tried making some calls. I'm just checking the video I shot of him," Burchill said as he tapped away on the screen of the smartphone. "Huh, there's nothing! I know I was recording him," he said as he scrolled through his pictures and videos stored on his smartphone.

"How did you get here? Were you all together?" Fulton asked Burchill referencing the group of seventy people.

Burchill was sporting a scowl as he continued to scroll through his pictures. "Get here?! I don't know where we are?! I don't know any of those people," he exclaimed as he motioned with his smartphone to the crowd of seventy people. "I keep thinking I must be dead, or I've been drugged, or maybe this is what crazy people experience. I don't think it's a dream because of the sensory detail–I smell the desert air, I hear you–ahh, my phone doesn't work!"

"You're not dead, drugged, or crazy. This is real," Fulton said to him.

"Do you know where we are?!" Burchill asked.

"The Ynez-Aztecan Reservation. We're in southeastern California," Fulton said.

"California?! I was at a conference in Vegas! I was listening to a presentation from some Caltech grad students on astrophysics when a blinding bright light flashed before me. A few seconds later, I was sitting over with those people listening to the most intriguing lecture on the history of the world," Burchill said as if he was retelling a story from a traffic accident.

"Do you know who is he is?" Fulton asked.

"Well, it appears that today I've experienced the warping of space-time, teleportation, and witnessed the midair birth of an extinct large mammal that hasn't been seen since the last Ice Age–I have a good idea who we're dealing with, but I would like to confer with him one more time to make sure–you know, that we're not all crazy," Burchill said with a smile. "While he's gone–I'm going down to the river to observe the woolly mammoth," he said as he touched Fulton's shoulder then squeezed his arm then felt the material of his shirt sleeve by rubbing it against the tips of his fingers. Fulton and Juan watched him as he walked away from them.

"Strange–very strange," Juan said.

"He's still wrestling with whether or not this is real. I must admit–I understand how he feels. Questioning your own sanity would be expected under these circumstances," Fulton said.

"I've been drugged–had some real crazy dreams and seen some horrible things. What I saw on the pier and what happened today– this is real. No doubt about it," Juan said as he turned to Pedro and Jim for confirmation.

"We saw what he did," Jim said as Pedro nodded his head.

"What is this about? Why is he here?" Pedro asked.

"Grow'in up–I always heard; when he comes back–it's judgement day," Teddy said as he looked at each of them then stopped at Fulton. "You know that," he said to Fulton.

"You're with the church, right?" Juan said to Fulton.

Fulton nodded and said, "The Archdiocese of New York."

"Yeah, I knew you were a priest. Pedro and me were altar boys at St. Luke's in East LA. I can spot you guys a mile away," Juan said. "So, why is he here?"

"I don't know. I wanted to ask him but each time–I'm overwhelmed by his holiness," Fulton said. "It's a feeling of complete peace."

"Could we be dead and you know–we're waiting at the pearly gates to get into heaven?" Jackie asked as she and Kimba stepped closer to Fulton.

"I don't have that pain–you know, the urge for something–not even for a cigarette," Kimba said as she rubbed her forearms.

The beat-up pickup truck drove toward the weathered buildings and past several people from the reservation who were running toward the river. Dakota and Tommy were back from their night of smuggling at the border. They sat in the truck watching people running past them.

"What's going on?" Tommy asked.

"They're crazy!" Dakota said as he opened the passenger door. "Hey, what's up?! Is Custer coming?!"

A middle-aged Ynez-Aztecan woman said as she walked toward the river, "There's a woolly mammoth down at the river!"

Dakota and Tommy looked at each other and laughed.

"I've got to check this out and get whatever they're smoking," Tommy said as he turned the key to shut-off the truck. They followed the woman down the embankment to the river.

The group of seventy people were situated into several clusters among the grove of trees along the riverbed. The woolly mammoth was by the river grabbing clumps of grass with its trunk and putting it into his mouth. Ava and Fulton were moving towards it when Dakota and Tommy appeared by the river.

"That's a freak'in woolly mammoth!" Tommy said to Dakota as he pulled out his smartphone and recorded it. "Dude, you've got your own Jurassic Park here."

The woolly mammoth raised his long thick trunk up in the air and blasted out a loud trumpet sound.

"I can't believe you didn't tell me!" Tommy said as continued recording with his smartphone.

"I've never seen this thing before," Dakota said wondering where it came from.

"This is so cool. Hey, I gotta bounce, but I'm coming back," Tommy said as he held his smartphone toward the creature.

Ava, holding a handful of long grass, stepped toward the woolly mammoth. "Here you go," Ava said as she held out the grass.

The woolly mammoth reached out with its trunk and carefully grabbed the grass from her. Ava laughed.

"Come on now, Ava. Step back and let it eat on its own," Fulton said as he put his hands-on Ava's shoulders and gently pulled her back away from the woolly mammoth. They walked over to Juan, Pedro, and the others.

"It hasn't stopped eating!" Jackie said.

"Isn't that why they're extinct? They ate everything in sight!" Kimba said.

"That's a myth that was applied to the extinction of the dinosaurs," Burchill said.

The woolly mammoth blasted another trumpet roar. Ava giggled and asked Jackie, "Did you see me feed him?"

"I did, honey. You're brave," Jackie said.

"Little girl," Burchill said.

"My name's Ava," she said.

"Ava, I saw you give–was that an iPod that you gave him?" Burchill asked.

"It was my dad's. Rabbouni likes my dad's playlist," Ava said.

"What type of music is it? What songs does, ah–Rabbouni like?" Burchill asked.

"Andre Bocelli, Mozart but mostly a lot of Elvis," Ava said.

"The King of Kings listens to the King of Rock and Roll, huh," Burchill said as he nodded his head. "Fascinating."

Duval Lewis was standing in the luxurious lobby of another Las Vegas hotel and casino. He was speaking with a security guard that was blocking the entrance to the casino.

"Do you think they'll open the casino today?" Lewis asked.

"Don't know. The IT guys are working on it. They're still trying to figure out what happened," the security guard said.

"The other casinos are closed too," Lewis said as his smartphone rang, and he pulled it out of his back pocket. He looked at the telephone number calling him then held up his index finger to the security guard before walking away from him. "Yeah, nothing new here. Haven't seen Fulton yet…What?! Send me the link now," Lewis said as he disconnected the call and opened his text message.

Lewis watched a video that was trending on several social media sites of the woolly mammoth by the river which then showed Ava feeding it grass with Fulton standing nearby her. "This was an hour ago!" Lewis exclaimed as he read the tag on the video feed. He slipped his smartphone into his back pocket and ran out of the casino.

Chapter Nine

Rabbouni returned from his walk. He was standing before a large crowd of people that included the group of seventy people, residents from the reservation, Ava, Fulton, and the others. They were all positioned under the shade from the grove of trees along the riverbed and remained silent while listening to Rabbouni. There were no offhand outbursts or unthoughtful questions from any of the diverse group of people as he spoke to them for two hours. It was more than that they knew not to interrupt him; it was the charismatic aura of him that captivated their attention and was reinforced by his spoken words.

"Each one of you have certain abilities that have been utilized to perpetuate life here. Jeanette, you spent most of your life as a teacher to five and six-year old children," Rabbouni said to a woman in her early sixties with short platinum blond hair. "You often think that you wasted your life when you compare it to some of your friends."

Jeanette looked down from embarrassment from that truth and the thought that everyone was looking at her. "Truly, you have been the most successful of all your friends. You helped so many children by creating the foundation for them to lead a life of love and truth. You will be rewarded far beyond any of your friends," Rabbouni said. He then turned to the crowd and said, "Forgiveness, mercy, and compassion are the key principles for a happy life. The people that extended forgiveness when they were wronged and provided mercy and compassion to those in despair are the blessed ones. You are all hungry and thirsty. Turn around and go sit down to eat and drink." The crowd of people turned around and saw rows of wooden picnic tables with wooden benches set up behind them beside the river. Each table, which could seat ten people, was covered with cooked fish, meat, and chicken, bowls of fresh fruit, vegetables, juices, and water.

"How was this set up right here without us knowing?" a man asked from the crowd. Many of them shook their heads in disbelief and wonder as they all moved toward the tables to sit down.

"Did your people set this up?" Juan asked Whitehorse who shook his head.

"We are not able to provide food like this. I'm just as surprised as you," Whitehorse said.

Ava was pouring water into cups and passing food out to people that were seated. Rabbouni watched her serve the people at the tables. He turned to Fulton, Teddy, Jackie, Pedro, and a few others and said, "See how that child serves them–complete self-sacrificing. That is what you all must do." Rabbouni then told them to sit down and eat with the others.

After everyone had their fill of food and drink, they stepped away from the banquet feast to listen to Rabbouni speak by the river. They sat on the ground or on rocks that were scattered about in the dry riverbed area while Rabbouni stood on a rock that jutted out from the embankment. He spoke to them with a powerful voice that permeated the air and could be heard clearly by everyone by the river.

"The mystery of life and all of creation as you know it–is not a mystery! The answer is simple. Many people know the answer and doubt it or reject it. You know the shape of a galaxy–its spiral shape looks like a spiral in a sea shell–you think that's a coincidence?! Most recognize the beginning as the Big Bang that created the universe and everything in it–what do you think created the Big Bang?! The amount of evidence that supports the truth of divine intervention is unlimited–eyes for humans and other living creatures to see was not an adaptation by nature no more than a machine being manufactured on its own. Some of the most obvious evidence of the divine is consciousness–the innate sense of good and evil and the generous gift of creativity that enables progress for humans," Rabbouni said.

The crowd of people listened to him with tears running down their faces. They were not sorry nor scared. They had an incredible euphoric feeling that was constant while they were in his presence. Anyone in the crowd of people that had a mental or physical health problem or even required medication for their respective condition–were completely healed.

The bright sun was still high in the sky above the desert. Duval Lewis was racing down the two-lane rural highway in his rental car heading to the Ynez-Aztecan Reservation. Even with the air-conditioning system turned to high cool, the broiling sun could be felt through the car windows. Lewis was talking on his smartphone as he drove along.

"This place is in the middle of nowhere–you wouldn't believe the traffic!" Lewis said.

A deep, strong voice from the telephone speaker could be heard, "That video is trending everywhere. You'll have a lot of company when you get there."

"I've passed TV news trucks, college kids jammed in cars, and there's even families on the road! They're all heading there, too!" Lewis exclaimed.

"Can't you find a faster route–take some short-cut through the desert?!"

"That posted video gave the GPS coordinates! Everyone knows how to get there. We can only hope for an accident to slow them down," Lewis said.

"They're all going to see the woolly mammoth–you're going for Fulton and that kid. So, let them take their selfies with some dumb hairy elephant! Keep focused on the story!" The distinct sound of the call being disconnected was heard. Lewis dropped his smartphone on the front passenger seat.

"Hmm, I'd still like to run these stupid pigs off the road just the same," Lewis said as he accelerated past an old sedan with a couple in the front seat and two young children in the back seat.

Lewis turned the steering wheel hard to the right, cutting off the car with the family in it. The old sedan swerved to the right as it abruptly slowed down as Lewis sped down the highway.

"Have a nice day!" Lewis yelled then laughed.

Lewis drove past an outcropping of rock as he travelled up a gradual incline on the road. As the car reached the crest of the hill, Lewis saw an expansive tract of the open desert located in a flat, desolate valley surrounded by distant red rock formations. He raced down the road into the valley. After a few minutes he noticed that there were several vehicles stopped in the road ahead of him. He drove right up to a parked RV that was towing a small car behind it. Lewis attempted to drive around it; however, another vehicle had already attempted to pass the RV but was now stopped in the oncoming traffic lane. Lewis shoved the gear shift into park, hopped out of the front seat, and walked up to the driver's side of the RV.

"What the heck's going on?! Why is everyone stopped?!" Lewis exclaimed to the driver who appeared concerned.

"Look!" the middle-aged RV driver said as he pointed down the road.

Lewis turned left and looked at the line of vehicles that were stopped in the road. There were people outside of their vehicles staring toward the horizon. Lewis focused past them. His eyes widened then he squinted as he tried to see what they were all looking at.

"What is everyone looking at?! What is it–a UFO?! You see any little green men?!" Lewis asked sarcastically to the driver of the RV.

"It's right out there in distance–it's a sandstorm!" the RV driver said.

A light brown line close to the ground stretched across the horizon that looked similar to a long border wall.

"What the hell does that mean?!" Lewis asked.

"It looks like it's coming this way," the RV driver said as some of his children within the vehicle commented that they were afraid.

"So, just roll up your windows and put your wipers on," Lewis said as he walked back to his car. "What a bunch of–go back to Walmart!" Lewis said as he hopped back into his car. The car tires screeched as he drove past the RV and went around the car blocking the road. He continued down the highway past dozens of cars and trucks that had stopped. Several vehicles started moving down the road after Lewis passed them.

After several minutes of driving the sky in front of him became darker. After dodging a few more stopped vehicles, Lewis looked up from the road to the horizon and saw that the sandstorm was now much closer and had grown considerably higher. It was a menacing sandstorm. "Whoa!" Lewis exclaimed as he continued driving forward.

The sandstorm looked like a gigantic superwave of rolling sand that was three hundred feet high and several miles wide. It was still a few miles away from him as he continued to drive along the highway. "Hmm, this is different," Lewis said.

The barometric pressure dropped as a sound similar to a freight train roared towards Lewis in his car. The sky became darker as grains of sand pelted the windshield as he drove along the road. Within a few minutes, the amount of sand hitting the windshield intensified. Lewis turned on the headlights and the windshield wipers as millions of jagged grains of sand scratched the glass and the outside of the car. He was frightened now.

The sun was blocked out as the sandstorm rolled over Lewis in his car. It was as if it was nighttime. He panicked when he could no longer see the road. Fearing that he may run into a parked car, Lewis swung the car to the left causing it to drive off the road. The car bottomed out in a drainage ditch then continued moving forward through the desert. He shifted his weight in the seat. "I can't see a damn thing!" he exclaimed as he squinted his eyes, gripped the steering wheel tightly, and leaned forward in an attempt to see better through the sand-blizzard conditions. He drove that way for a few minutes but slowed down as the car passed through more loose sand and dirt that was being dropped by the sandstorm. The car stopped moving forward as the wheels spun in the loose ground. The whining sound of the rubber tires spinning and the howling noise of the sandstorm reverberated inside the small car.

Lewis threw the gear shift in reverse attempting to get back onto the road. The tires spun into the sand as the car dropped lower into a freshly carved rut. He tried rocking the car back and forth by slamming the car into reverse then back to drive while stomping on the accelerator. "Son-of-a…!" Lewis exclaimed as he pounded the steering wheel with his fist and repeated the futile exercise of rocking the car forward and backwards until the spinning tires no longer were kicking up sand. The front wheels were now fully dug into the sand. Lewis looked outside through the windshield and into the sandstorm, off in the distance some several miles away, he saw a strange red pulsating column. "What's that?!" Lewis said as he tried to discern what he was looking at.

The red pulsating column grew much larger and changed into an orange-red twisting column that stretched toward the sky then began to bend and zig-zag across the desert floor. "What the hell is this?!" Lewis exclaimed as it moved to within a mile of him. Dozens of lightning discharges could be seen within the massive twisting column. As this strange phenomenon moved closer to the car, he saw that it was a tornado of fire heading right for him. He struggled to open the car door to run away but the sand outside had risen to the door handles preventing his escape. He screamed for help as the huge tornado of fire filled his view through the windshield. A bolt of lightning erupted from the twisting fire tornado and struck the car. Inside the car, there was a pinkish flash of blinding light then followed by a scream from Lewis.

Moments later, the darkness from the sandstorm lightened up to a brown haze then blotches of blue sky appeared. Lewis' car roof had been ripped open down the middle by the lightning strike. The interior of the car was now exposed to the blazing sun. Lewis was lying across the front seat. He opened his eyes and wondered if he was alive. He moved his hands then pushed himself upright in the driver's seat. Lewis was shaking with fear as he climbed up onto the seat, then onto the dashboard and out onto the hood of the car. He was astonished from the aftermath of the sandstorm.

Lewis stood on the hood of the rental car which seemed to be a tiny island of safety in the desert. He saw that the rental car was surrounded by sand and gravel measuring three feet deep and out as far as he could see. Lewis stepped down from the hood of the car and began walking toward the closest outcropping of rock. He decided to walk in that particular direction from his gut feeling.

The hot sun beat down on him. He was thirsty and tired but continued to walk through the desert.

Tommy walked up to Dakota who was standing near the crowd of people which included the group of seventy and the others.

"Hey, didn't expect you back so soon," Dakota said.

"Yeah, me too! I ran into a freak sandstorm that covered the highway–so I turned around. But I have to show you something," Tommy said as he held out his smartphone for Dakota to see it. "I posted your pet mammoth taking a bubble bath down at the river– my phone has blown up! Check this out–six million views!" Tommy laughed as he played the video showing Ava feeding the woolly mammoth.

Burchill stepped over to see the video. "You were able to get cell phone coverage here?" he asked as he watched the video.

"No. I left and was all the way out to the state highway before I could use it," Tommy answered Burchill. "I still can't believe it; and I saw it!" Tommy said to Dakota commenting on the woolly mammoth in the video. "Where is it now?!"

"Down by the river. It's still eating," Dakota said.

"You got a million hits on that video?!" Burchill asked.

"Six million hits and still going," Tommy said as he laughed and held his hand out for a high-five from Dakota. "I lost cell coverage coming back here–I bet it's ten million now!"

"I would think that it's passed that by a considerable factor. Unfortunately, it will create great interest which will result in mobs of people coming here," Burchill said.

"Yeah, I guess. There were some people that saw my post that said they were going to drive out here. But you know how people talk–they're so full of it," Tommy said as he laughed.

"This is much different–this is an extinct mammal. We need to expect that a lot of people are coming here to see it," Burchill said as he turned to Whitehorse who had been listening to the conversation.

"Not after that sandstorm!" Tommy exclaimed.

"What sandstorm?!" Dakota asked.

"Oh, there was a huge sandstorm! The highway is covered with sand–like two feet deep! Nobody's coming here for a while–unless they have a camel," Tommy said.

"This is historic news! It will attract national and international media and many people," Burchill said with concern for the woolly mammoth. "However, under the circumstances, there is a person among us who can make anything happen. I guess, there's probably no need for us to worry," he said as he walked away.

Away from the larger crowd of assembled people, Rabbouni was teaching a smaller group about life. The smaller group consisted of Fulton, Teddy, Juan, Pedro, Jackie, Kimba, and Jim who were sitting on the ground listening intently to Rabbouni. He told them each in great detail about their own lives. He explained to them about free will and why they made certain decisions in their respective lives and what particular ramifications those decisions had on them and other people. They had many questions for him: what had happened to loved ones; why did a person do something that was hurtful; why did a bad thing happened to them? Rabbouni answered their questions and explained to each of them–their arc of life.

"Does this mean our lives are over," Jackie asked with tears running down her face.

"You will never know the exact time life here ends–but you will be reborn in another place for eternity," Rabbouni said.

Whitehorse and another person walked towards the small group sitting around Rabbouni. Whitehorse went ahead by himself to speak to Rabbouni.

"The person you told me about is here," Whitehorse said.

"Send him to me," Rabbouni said.

Whitehorse walked back and sent the person forward to see Rabbouni. As the person got closer to the small group, Fulton recognized him. It was Duval Lewis. Fulton leaned over to Rabbouni and whispered to him, "This man has done some bad things…" Fulton said then stopped midsentence when Rabbouni made eye contact with him. Fulton thought how Rabbouni knew everything about everyone and more importantly that he–Fulton should not be judging anyone. Fulton looked down being ashamed of himself as Lewis approached them.

Lewis stopped several feet from Rabbouni and fell to his knees.

"I've come here as you told me to," Lewis cried out to Rabbouni and leaned forward to the ground. "I beg you for forgiveness! I'm truly sorry for the terrible things I have done to people! Please forgive me!"

"Your evil lies created an environment of division and hatred among people. You will only be able to speak the truth from now on. Sit with the others," Rabbouni said to Lewis who then sat down with the small group.

Whitehorse stepped closer to the small group and waited for Rabbouni's attention. Rabbouni turned and motioned for him to speak.

"A video of the mammoth has reached the public. Many people are coming here," Whitehorse said.

"They will not be able to get here today and tomorrow they will never find it," Rabbouni said.

Chapter Ten

Early morning on Friday, the traffic was already heavy in Midtown Manhattan. A middle-aged nun dressed in black with a black habit on her head walked quickly through the crowded sidewalk. She had rosary beads wrapped around her folded hands and prayed silently as she moved along. She entered the old St. Monika's Hospital located a few blocks from Central Park.

The nun took the elevator to the fifth floor and walked down the hall to the children's wing for the most unfortunate patients. Another nun was frantically pushing a large metal hospital crib on wheels into the hallway that was overloaded with children with various disabilities and terminal illnesses. Both nuns looked at each as several children moaned from their respective health condition.

"Sister Marie, I've come to help," Sister Louise said as she put her hands on the hospital crib.

"Did you have the dream, too?!" Sister Marie asked.

Sister Louise nodded her head and said, "I did. And I know where to take them."

"Me, too."

"But, there's so many children. How are we going to move them all?" Sister Louise asked.

"We'll just put as many as we can into these cribs then tie them together and push them. And then one of us can go back and get more while the other one waits with the children," Sister Marie said.

A man in his early sixties with a weathered face appeared around the corner from the elevator. He was dressed in a dark-blue long sleeve shirt and matching pants with a name tag that read: Kern –

Facilities.

The two nuns turned toward him.

"Good morning, Kern," the sisters said.

"Good morning, sisters. I've come to help," Kern said to them.

"Did you have the dream?" Sister Louise asked him.

"I did. I wasn't sure at first, but I came to do it," Kern said.

At that moment a frail woman in her early sixties came around the

corner.

"Honey?!" the woman exclaimed.

Kern turned around and walked over to her. "It's okay. I'm here,"

he said to her as he took her hand and walked her over to the nuns.

"This is my beautiful wife and best friend. Her name is Ruth. She

has dementia. I'm going to help, but I'm taking my Ruth with me,"

Kern said.

The nuns smiled at him.

At 9:00 AM that same morning in the Manhattan Family Courthouse, Sister Carmella and Monica Moore were sitting at the defense table in the courtroom. Ms. Pratt and the two attorneys from the City Attorney's Office were at the prosecutor's table. Ms. Pratt had her strange wide-grin on her face as she stared over at Sister Carmella. The court clerk came into the courtroom and stood before the judge's bench.

"Attention everyone! Please listen to the following announcement: Judge Martin Silver will not be presiding in this courtroom today. He will be out on medical leave until further notice. Today's court proceedings will be handled by the Honorable Judge Henry Elam. All rise!" the court clerk said.

The people in the courtroom stood up as Judge Elam entered and sat down at the judge's bench. He was in his fifties with a pencil-thin mustache and a close-cropped afro with a distinguished blend of gray through it.

"Please be seated. Court is now in session," the court clerk said.

Monica Moore leaned over to Sister Carmella to comment about the change in presiding judges. "This judge is known to be very tough," she whispered then wrinkled her nose and pursed her lips with concern.

"I'm not worried," Sister Carmella said.

The judge reviewed the case summary before him.

"Good morning, everyone. I've read the briefing submission from the City Attorney's Office and the one from the defense and I've read Judge Silver's notes on the case. The case before this court is simple. We have a guardian issue for a juvenile, a contempt of court charge, and a possible restraining order," Judge Elam said.

The two attorneys from the City Attorney's Office nodded their heads as Ms. Pratt smirked then revealed a big toothy smile that was not appropriate for this situation. Meanwhile, Monica Moore and Sister Carmella looked forward as they listened to the judge.

"After careful review of the facts presented, this court declares that while Mrs. Margaret Rose is incapacitated, or if she subsequently dies from her illness, that the responsibilities of guardianship for her daughter Ava Marie Rose are granted to Sister Carmella who is the Principal of Fontbonne Academy in Manhattan, New York," Judge Elam said.

"This is an outrage!" Ms. Pratt screeched.

Judge Elam banged his gavel on the bench and sternly said, "Order in the court! Mr. Prosecutor, I strongly advise that you get her under control." The judge held eye contact with the older prosecutor until he leaned over to Ms. Pratt.

"Just sit there and be quiet," the older prosecutor said to her.

The judge cleared his throat and said, "I understand there is a next of kin–a great-aunt; which there is no history of a relationship with the child. A guardian with a healthy relationship is key to the child's well-being. The child has such a relationship at the school and under the circumstances would not have to suffer from the negative impact to her life from being moved 3,000 miles away from her friends and school. The next item is the contempt of court issue; this court finds no grounds that the court order was willingly violated by Sister Carmella. So, the charge of contempt of court is dismissed with prejudice."

Ms. Pratt gasped then moved in her seat as she gripped the wooden armrests of the chair as if she was about to stand up. The older prosecutor leaned over toward her and said, "Stop it! Control yourself!"

The judge banged his gavel again. "Order! Officer, please have some restraints brought into the court room," Judge Elam said, sternly.

The senior court officer motioned to another court officer who was standing by the double wooden doors who immediately slipped out of the courtroom. The senior court officer stepped closer to the prosecutor's table and waited for further direction from the judge.

"Now, regarding the last issue of a restraining order. After reading the testimony from the police officers at the scene and the other witnesses, I have to say that I was completely shocked at your behavior–Ms. Pratt!" the judge said.

Ms. Pratt's face contorted into a strange look then changed into one of her toothy wide-grins.

"I don't think it's funny at all. In fact, this court will issue a restraining order against you–Ms. Pratt. This court orders that you shall not go within 1,000 feet of the Fontbonne Academy School."

Ms. Pratt let out a grunt as the court officer returned with another court officer who was holding handcuffs attached to chains and a leather gag for her mouth. The two court officers stood several feet from the prosecutor's table and looked over to the judge for instructions.

"Your behavior in the school was unprofessional, reckless, and an abuse of power. You terrorized those children, and in my opinion, you are a threat to the public."

Ms. Pratt grunted again.

"Your aggressive nature and abuse of power regarding this case compels me to write out a complaint to the mayor and advise that you are removed from the department!"

Ms. Pratt let out a louder prolonged groan.

"That's it! Officers, remove her from this courtroom and hold her downstairs until the City Attorney calls me regarding this case!" the judge exclaimed.

The judge turned to the two attorneys from the City Attorney's Office who were sitting at the edge of their seats with their hands folded on the table. "Do you have anything to say?" the judge asked.

The older prosecutor shook his head and said, "No, your honor. Nothing more from the City Attorney's Office. Thank you, judge."

Judge Elam looked over to Monica Moore who was in disbelief of what had just happened in the courtroom. She expected that the court would decide in the favor of the city and child services. "And you–counselor, are we good?" the judge asked.

"Yes, your honor. Nothing more from the defense. Thank you, judge," Monica Moore said quickly fearing that the judge might change his mind.

"Great. Okay, I will issue the necessary orders this morning. That's all. Thank you," the judge said as he stood up and left the bench.

"All rise!" exclaimed the senior court officer.

The people stood up as the judge left the courtroom. Monica Moore looked over to Sister Carmella who flashed a warm smile at her. A court officer walked over to Sister Carmella at the defense table. "Sister, the judge would like to speak with you in his chambers," he said.

Monica Moore was surprised with the judge's request and looked over to Sister Carmella, "I'll go with you," she said.

"No. The judge wants to see her–alone," the court officer said, firmly.

"Don't worry; I'll be fine," she said as she walked toward the judge's chambers with the court officer leading the way.

Sister Carmella entered the dark-wood paneled office that had a high ceiling which made the room seem larger than it was. Judge Elam was standing in front of an old mahogany executive desk. The court officer closed the office door leaving Sister Carmella alone with the judge. She looked over to the judge who had a large beaming smile across his face.

"Sister, it's been such a long time," he said as he walked over and hugged her as one would do with a close relative.

"I told you that you would be a judge someday," she said as she wiped a tear from her eye, and he moved back a step from her.

"I'm here because you believed in me when I didn't," he said as tears welled up in his eyes.

"We all need some help some time in our lives, and the Lord always works for us–in small ways and sometimes in big ways. The key is to be a good-loving person that is obedient to God. And that's you–Henry; you were as a young boy and you are as a grown man," she said with a warm smile. "Thank you for protecting Ava."

"On the contrary, thank you for protecting her and all the many others over the years," he said.

Sister Carmella had left Monica Moore at the bottom of the stone steps of the courthouse. She was praying as she walked along the crowded sidewalk. The deep sound of a ram's horn being blown was heard down the busy avenue while it echoed off the tall buildings. Sister Carmella abruptly stopped walking and turned her head attempting to hear where the sound had come from. Several other people further down the street had also stopped and were looking around as if they too would be able to see where the strange noise originated. The constant background noise of car and truck horns replaced the momentary silence. Then the low deep sound of the ram's horn being blown grew louder; quickly drowning out the car and truck horns.

Sister Carmella listened to the long blast from the ram's horn as its baritone sound lingered in the air. She determined that it was coming from the next block over to the east. She turned and walked toward it as several others on the crowded street did the same. Each subsequent blast from the ram's horn seemed to last longer than the previous one. As Sister Carmella walked along the busy street toward the sound of the ram's horn, more people headed in the same direction while many others walked away from it.

As she walked to the end of the street and stood at the intersection, she looked across Fifth Avenue that ran along the eastside of Central Park. Hundreds of people were hurrying around the stopped vehicles as they crossed the street into the open wrought iron gates of the famous city park. Sister Carmella held the wooden cross that hung from her neck in both hands as she whispered several phrases while walking across the multiple lanes of stopped traffic. Some people had abandoned their cars and some left their trucks while others stayed in their vehicles blowing their horns and yelling for people to come back.

"What the HELL are you doing?! Come on! Move your DAMN car!" said the driver of a small yellow minivan that highlighted quick delivery service in large print on its side doors.

Sister Carmella blended in with the crush of people pouring into the park. Even though it was a very large number of people, they all moved in an orderly fashion without pushing or aggressively pressing forward. They were all going to the same area—the wide-open space covered in green grass. However, it was now filled with people and something was very different with the topography of this field. Since it was created in the 19th Century, it was a relatively flat open space surrounded by trees. Strangely, a large rectangular block of blue granite that stood thirty feet high and ten feet across was now standing at the end of the open field. The sides of the granite block were polished smooth and sheer from the top edge to the ground. There was no way to climb it.

The crowd of people were moving toward the granite block. They were staring at it and mumbling to themselves and others nearby. The grouping of the people in the open field was obvious. The people closest to the granite block appeared to be everyday people—some wore modest clothing and many others had much less since they were poor. The people with far better financial means were in the back of the crowd along the perimeter of the open field.

"What is this about?!" someone yelled from the back of the crowd.

"How did that get here?!" someone else yelled referencing the granite block.

Many in the crowd told them to be quiet and wait.

There were people outside of Central Park that were trying to get through one of the many openings to the park. They were not able to walk onto the sidewalk bordering the park. As soon as they stepped from the street asphalt onto the concrete sidewalk; they would fall backwards to the street, landing among the stopped vehicles. They were unable to move their arms and legs. There were many celebrities, politicians, and affluent people who were laying on the ground in the street demanding entry based on their respective importance and status.

"I've been nominated for two Emmys and a Golden Globe. I've got ten million followers. Someone carry me in!" the twentysomething actress demanded.

Twenty yards away, the Mayor of New York City was on the ground. His long arms and legs were motionless. However, his mouth never stopped moving. "I'm the Mayor of New York City! I should be in there! Pick me up, NOW!" he demanded. His two aides attempted to lift him, but they fell to ground as well and were unable to move themselves. An older man that would be recognized around the world for his business acumen laid on the ground not able to move. "I've pledged to give more than a hundred billion dollars away when I die! Someone help me!" he said knowing that his fortune would be going to a family foundation that would leak out small drips of financial donations to charities or questionable causes.

The pleasant scent of wet sage and eucalyptus filled the air. The sound of the ram's horn blasted out for a longer time and was by far louder than previously. Some of the people standing in the park covered their ears as others looked around expecting something to happen. A violet-purple streak came down from high above in the sky at a forty-five-degree angle that stretched down to the top of the granite block. The people let out a loud gasp that swept across the whole crowd as a man that was dressed in a blinding white robe appeared on the top of the granite block–it was Rabbouni. Meanwhile, unbeknownst to the crowd, a group of people that numbered more than seventy people appeared around the base of the granite block. The newly arrived group of people included Ava, Fulton, Teddy, Pedro, Juan, and the others that were assembled from the reservation.

Ava looked at the crowd of people around them. She stood beside Fulton and was surrounded by Pedro, Juan, and the others.

"Where are we?" Jim asked.

"Central Park–New York City," Fulton said.

"How did we get here? I woke-up in the middle of the night–we were still at the Indian reservation–I'm sure of it!" Burchill exclaimed.

Pedro, Juan, and Jim looked at Fulton for an answer.

"Hopefully, he's going to tell us what this is all about," Fulton said.

"This may be the last day for everyone," Teddy said.

The crowd of thousands of people erupted with a gasp as Rabbouni stepped to the edge of the granite block. Then everyone went silent and stood completely still. There was no background noise whatsoever.

"The words you will hear today were said two thousand years ago. They were instructions for all men and women living life here," Rabbouni said. His words projected to the thousands of people present and could be clearly heard by those standing at the very edge of the open field. There were no speakers or microphones to broadcast his voice. Yet, his voice projected at a volume that everyone in the open field could hear every word he spoke.

Broadcast news trucks had pulled over at various locations around Central Park. Many of the cameramen climbed onto the news trucks and set up their large high-resolution digital video cameras on tripods while others rushed to the sidewalk. All of them were determined to catch some footage of whatever was happening in Central Park to feed the endless news cycle that the public consumed. However, only a small group of reporters and cameramen were able to walk across the sidewalk and pass through the wrought iron gates into Central Park.

Those reporters and cameramen positioned themselves among the crowd and pointed their video cameras at Rabbouni who was standing on the granite block.

"Many people buy lottery tickets everyday hoping for a great wealth of money. It would be far better for them to pray every day for blessings here and a much greater reward for all eternity," Rabbouni said while everyone in the crowd was silent and listened to him. "Too many people are focused on themselves and only speak lies. Lies are words that lead to evil. Everyone wants clean air and clean water. Everyone should only use words that are clean of lies and deceit; anything else is evil. Humankind has been imperfect since their creation. And there have been times in its history that they have been punished to bring them back to follow the Almighty's instructions. Even though God Almighty has created everything in the universe; many people still doubt his existence, refuse to follow his Words and even punish his believers. Humankind has reached a point where something must be done to change the way people behave and act toward one another or everything here must end. Signs or miracles don't change human behavior," Rabbouni said as he looked up to the clear blue sky. Moments later, clouds rolled in then changed into strange patterns that turned the sky gray then blood red then a purplish-red. The crowd quietly gasped in fear. "The nonbelievers and evildoers would say that it was just a weather event. To get the masses to respond–it must be something on a grand scale. I truly tell you the Lord Almighty is not pleased with the way people behave to each other," Rabbouni said then a bolt of lightning splintered across the sky followed by a large boom of thunder. The crowd gasped louder and some screamed. The morning sky became dark as night then a moment later millions of stars twinkled across the blackness above the crowd. People screamed and cried out for mercy.

Ava was scared and reached for Fulton's hand. He was startled by her touch as he was fixated on Rabbouni. He looked down at her and squeezed her hand.

"What's happening?" Ava asked.

"I'm not sure. But I know you don't have to worry," Fulton said to her as he continued to watch Rabbouni.

Then in an instant the sun reappeared in the sky which caused everyone in the crowd to close their eyes and look away from the blinding light.

While Ava looked down on the ground a small black cat with a clipped ear appeared at her feet.

"Mumma Cat! Is that you?! How did you get here," Ava asked as she bent down to rub the back of her neck. The black cat slipped away in between the crowd of people. Ava followed her moving away from Fulton and the others. The black cat continued to stay just a few feet from Ava's grasp as they moved through the crowd away from the granite block. "Mumma Cat, come here!" Ava yelled as she pushed her way through the crowd trying to get the small black cat. There were so many people in the field it was difficult for Ava to catch the cat. Each attempt to grab her was foiled by the cat slipping away between someone's legs. Ava chased after the cat. She saw the cat run out of the field and through a park gate.

Ava walked onto the sidewalk outside of Central Park. The black cat was standing at the edge of the curb looking back toward Ava.

"Mumma Cat! Come here!" Ava said as the cat let out a meow. She ran to the cat who leaped into the street as Ava touched her fur. Ava followed the cat into the street. There was a loud thump then Ava was thrown into the air as an old beat-up red pickup truck overloaded with construction equipment rumbled on as she fell to the pavement with a dull thud. Her small body laid barefoot and motionless in the street. Her shoes were almost thirty feet away at the actual spot where she was struck. On the opposite side of the street, the handsome man dressed in the dark-gray suit from the Venice Fishing Pier turned and walked away.

Meanwhile, a tear ran down Rabbouni's face as he continued speaking to the crowd.

"I'm saddened that many people have turned away from following the words and instructions from the Father Almighty– with that will come a judgement!" Rabbouni said.

At that moment, outside of Central Park on the street, a number of famous celebrities, wealthy people, and certain government officials were struggling on the pavement. They continued to yell out for people to serve them and bring them into the park. As they squirmed and wriggled about, many of them experienced a strange transformation in which their hands and feet changed into cloven hooves. While others grew curved horns several inches long from the top of their heads and their faces morphed into a goat's nose and mouth.

Rabbouni raised his hand to the crowd of people.

"You are all here to change the others from their sinful ways. In a few moments, you will be the ones to set the example for love, joy, peace, patience, kindness, generosity, faithfulness, gentleness, and self-control," Rabbouni said as a golden light emitted from him and spread out into the crowd of people. It looked like a shockwave as it passed through the people. The crowd let out a gentle gasp then stood silent.

"Always remember the two most important rules: love thy neighbor; and love God Almighty with your mind, heart, and soul! Now, all of you–go and spread the Word and save your brothers and sisters," Rabbouni commanded them then a blinding white light emitted from him then he disappeared. The crowd began to move about and speak fluently to each other in foreign languages that they previously did not understand nor speak. They all commented on how they felt unusually healthy and full of energy. Moreover, people that were ill stated that they knew that they were now free of any illness. People that were in wheelchairs or struggled to be mobile were completely healed and moved freely. Once they realized that Rabbouni was not coming back, they filed out of Central Park and went their separate ways. The pleasant scent in the park was changed to the dirty pollutant-filled air of the city. Reporters and television crews tried to interview as many people as possible that walked out of the park.

"What happened in there? What did you see?" a television reporter asked an Asian man that walked through one of the opened wrought iron gates.

As the man talked about Rabbouni, the reporter became skeptical of the man's testimony.

"What did he look like?" the reporter asked.

"He looked like me," the Asian man said.

Another person that came out of the park was asked the same question by the reporter. This person was a black man that said that Rabbouni looked like him. Still another person who had strong Peruvian features said that Rabbouni had looked like him. After several more ethnically diverse people made the same statement, the reporter concluded that this whole experience in Central Park was an elaborate hoax or some type of large-scale deception conducted by a sophisticated group of people or government entity.

A young cameraman came out of the park holding his large video camera. He rushed over to the news truck and yelled for his colleagues. The older cameraman on the truck looked down as the driver hopped out of the truck.

"I've got it all, right here! You won't believe what happened in there!" the young cameraman said as he fumbled with the buttons on his digital video camera. He pressed the reverse button and flipped up the small LCD screen for his colleagues to see the footage he had recorded.

"Wait till you see the huge block of granite! When he first appeared–did you see the lighting?! How about when he made it nighttime?!" the young cameraman exclaimed.

"Take it easy, kid! What are you talking about?!" the older cameraman said who was standing on the news truck.

"Didn't you see the lightning go across the sky?! When he turned day into night?! All of those stars! Then boom–it was daytime again! It was incredible!" the young cameraman exclaimed.

The driver and the older cameraman looked at each other then laughed.

"You okay? I mean–you on something?" the older cameraman asked with a chuckle.

"Look at this!" the young cameraman said as he pressed the play button on his camera.

They watched the video coverage which showed the crowd of people but when it panned over to where the granite block was or when Rabbouni had spoken to the people, it was missing from the footage.

"Yeah, great. You got a large group of people in Central Park. That happens any weekend here," the older cameraman said as he rolled his eyes and smirked to the driver.

"It's not here! Damn it! I know what I saw," the young cameraman yelled as he frantically fast forwarded the footage in short clips desperately checking what he had recorded. "Didn't you guys see when it went pitch-black?!" the young cameraman said.

The older cameraman and the driver looked at each other and laughed.

Chapter Eleven

Meanwhile, at the nearest hospital to Central Park, ten metal

gurneys on wheels were lined up against the wall in the rear

hallway. Each gurney had a recently deceased person on it that was

covered with a white hospital sheet from head to toe. The deceased

were waiting to be transported by various funeral homes for final

arrangements. At the end of the hallway were two windowless

doors that opened to a loading area. Rabbouni emerged from the

two closed doors passing through the steel then stepped into the

hallway. As he walked past the first gurney that had a dead person

on it; there was movement under the sheet. Rabbouni continued to

walk down the hallway past the next gurney; that dead body stirred under the sheet. He walked by the third gurney and the same movement occurred for that dead body. Rabbouni walked past the fourth gurney but there was no movement under that sheet. He continued to walk down the hallway passing the remaining six gurneys with a dead body on each; there was movement from all but two bodies. As Rabbouni past the last dead body lying on the gurney, he turned to the right towards the stone tile wall and walked into the wall. As he disappeared into the wall, seven of the ten dead bodies that were laying on the gurneys sat up while the sheets covering them slowly slipped down from their faces.

In a crowded operating room in the hospital, three nurses and two doctors were frantically working on Ava. The doctors and nurses were speaking over the competing noise from the various electronic monitors that chirped out Ava's vital signs. The loud piercing sound of the alarm signaling that Ava's heart was now flatlining bounced off the sterile blank walls. The medical team changed tactics.

"We've got cardiac arrest! Let's go!" the middle-aged doctor ordered as a nurse handed him two paddles connected to tightly coiled electric cables. Another nurse pulled Ava's loose-fitting shirt from her left shoulder then quickly smeared a gel on Ava's chest above her heart.

"Charging–500!" yelled one of the nurses as the middle-aged doctor pressed the paddles down onto Ava's chest.

"Clear!" the middle-aged doctor said as several hundred volts of electricity surged into Ava's body which caused her little frame to momentarily lift up from the hospital gurney. The high-pitched whining sound of the heart monitor continued to blare a flatline warning. "Again!" the middle-aged doctor ordered.

"Charging–500!" yelled the nurse.

"Clear!" said the middle-aged doctor who then fired the electric charge into Ava's chest which caused her body to jump up again from the gurney. The doctor looked over to the monitor to see if there was any heart pulse. The high-pitched warning sound of

Ava's heart flatlining continued. The doctor ordered the nurse to prepare for another charge. Ava's motionless body leaped again from the gurney.

"No response," the other doctor said as the nurses and the two doctors looked down at Ava who was still barefoot.

"I'm calling time of death," the middle-aged doctor said as he looked up to the clock on the opposite wall. At that moment, from that same wall, a golden light emitted from it followed by Rabbouni who stepped into the operating room. The nurses and doctors gasped at the site of Rabbouni. One of the nurses and the other doctor disappeared from the room; the only thing remaining were their light green hospital clothing and operating masks which were on the floor in a pile at the exact location they were last seen.

Rabbouni, surrounded by a light-golden aura, walked toward the hospital gurney where Ava's lifeless body laid. The middle-aged doctor and the remaining nurses watched from the opposite side of the gurney. Rabbouni stood by the gurney and looked down at

Ava's body. "Ava, wake up," he said then at that moment Ava's eyes opened wide. "Come with me, my child," Rabbouni said as he reached down to her, Ava got up onto her knees and reached up to him as he lifted her from the gurney. Ava rested her head on his shoulder as he turned away from the gurney and walked back toward the wall. Rabbouni and Ava both disappeared into the wall.

Ava was lying beside her mother, outside of the bed covers, on the hospital bed. They were both asleep while a muffled commotion was coming from the corridor. The door opened then a nurse rushed into the room. She stopped at the large double window and pulled diagonally down on the nylon cord which pulled the metal louvered shade up until it clicked into place. The bright sunshine filled the room as Ava and her mother woke up from their sleep.

"You must see this! Take a look!" the nurse exclaimed as she looked back toward the window. "Isn't that beautiful?!" the nurse said.

Ava and her mother slipped off the bed and walked over toward the nurse. They looked out the window.

"It's a rainbow!" Ava exclaimed.

It was a vibrantly colored rainbow that arched across the city sky.

"It's amazing," Ava's mother said. "It's pulsating!"

"Rabbouni said that a rainbow means that God has done something for you!" Ava exclaimed.

The commotion in the hallway became louder with gleeful cheers. "What's going on out there?" Ava's mother asked.

"God has done something–everyone in the hospital has been cured!" the nurse said.

Ava's mother thought about her condition. She did feel better. She looked to the nurse for confirmation. "How do you know?!" she asked with great desperation.

"You look healthy. We'll send you for testing just to make sure. But everyone we send for testing comes back cured of whatever illness they had," the nurse said as she put a hand on Ava's mother shoulder. "I'm sure it will be the same for you."

Ava's mother cried as she bent down and hugged Ava.

"Don't cry, Mommy. See the rainbow. God did something for you–you're not sick anymore," Ava said.

Made in the USA
Middletown, DE
19 July 2021

44211556R00158